I0785409

The Prom Night Hitchhiker

Secrets of the South, Book 2

Cynthia Hickey

ISBN-13:978-1-968792-15-2

There's an Arkansas urban legend about Highway 365.

Years ago, a young man was driving down Arkansas 365 south of Little Rock when he saw a young girl on the roadside. He offered to give her a lift and draped his coat over her shoulders because she was shivering and soaked from the rain. She gave him directions to her house. When the young man got out of the car and walked around to the other side to help her out of her seat, no one was there.

Confused, the man walked up to the house and knocked on the door. A woman answered, and he explained what had occurred. She said, "That young girl was my daughter, who was killed years ago on this very day. She hitchhikes back home once a year." The young man then drove to the cemetery to see the young girl's grave. To his surprise, he found his coat draped over her tombstone.

This is my fictional telling of this mystery.

Prologue

Ethan Duvall loosened his tie and draped it over the tuxedo jacket on the passenger seat of his rusty Ford truck. Prom night hadn't been exactly as he'd envisioned it. No steamy prolonged time spent with his date, Peggy, who had decided to leave with another guy. Nope, not the senior prom he'd hoped for.

He switched on his windshield wipers as the rain increased. As he rounded a curve, he slammed on his brakes. A teenage girl in a filmy white dress, bare feet pale against the asphalt, seemed to glow in the moonlight. Her long, dark hair hung in damp strands around her face. She wrapped her arms around her middle as if she tried to warm herself.

She lifted her face, sending him an imploring look. That settled it. He set the truck in park, sent his brother a text saying he'd be late because he needed to give a girl a ride, and then grabbed his tuxedo jacket before exiting the truck.

"You okay, miss?" He glanced around to see whether she was alone. "Do you need a ride?"

"Yes, please. I need to get home."

He draped his jacket around her shoulders and helped her into the passenger seat. She introduced herself as Lilly and gave him an address a couple of miles away. "My date left me to walk home."

"Sounds like my date." He glanced at her feet. "Where are your shoes?"

"I left them behind a few miles back." She gave him a smile that chilled his heart. A smile that didn't reach her eyes.

"You're lucky I came by. This highway doesn't get much traffic at night."

"Lucky…" Her tone faded off on a whisper before she spoke again. "Do you believe in fate?"

He hesitated. "I…guess so. I mean, sometimes things happen that feel like they were meant to. Why?"

"No reason. I sometimes wonder if things would've been better if I'd made a different choice."

Ethan's unease deepened. "What do you mean?"

"Nothing. There's my house." A small, weathered cottage nestled among the trees. "Thank you for the loan of your jacket." She started to hand it back.

"Keep it. I'll come by tomorrow to pick it up." He watched as she rounded the cottage, then disappeared around the corner. "Pretty girl, but very strange." Maybe they could talk more tomorrow. Since Peggy ditched him, a new girl might be just the thing he needed, except that something about Lilly didn't seem right.

Ethan stopped at the cottage again the next morning on his way to work. He rapped three times on the door with peeling blue paint, then stepped back.

A gray-haired woman, eyes bright and sharp, answered. "Yeah?"

"I'm here to get my jacket back from Lilly."

She frowned. "Lilly? What kind of game are you playing? She died years ago and only comes home once a year."

What? His mouth dropped open. "No, I gave her a ride here last night."

"As someone always does when she returns." She jerked her head toward the back of the house. "See for yourself. Her grave is out back." She slammed the door.

Ethan jumped from the porch and searched for the house address in his phone. The map app didn't show a residence at this location. Could things get any weirder?

He located Lilly's grave near the edge of an old cemetery beneath the sprawling branches of a magnolia tree. The headstone was weathered but legible, and the date of her death, fifty years ago, clutched his heart with an icy fist. If Lilly was dead, then who had he picked up last night, and why was his jacket draped over the tombstone?

A rustle sounded behind him as he reached for his jacket. He whipped around.

Five women in white gowns stood at the edge of the tree line. They moved toward him with measured footsteps, all in sync, their intense gazes focused on him. Ethan made a mad dash for his truck only to find his path blocked by more women. One approached him and blew him a kiss, sending a fine dust into his face.

He crumpled to the ground, and the world went dark.

Chapter One

Pressley Taylor sat with her feet propped on top of her desk, a cup of coffee in her hand, and watched the rain leave rivulets on the front window of Hudson and Taylor Investigations in the quaint town of Redwood, Arkansas. Since the successful solving of a cold case from the 1940s, business had been good, made even better by her partnership with Jackson. He seemed content as a PI, something she'd worried about after he left the Texarkana Police Department and followed her to Northern Arkansas.

"What's on your mind?" Jackson gave a dimpled smile from his desk. "Enjoying a quiet rainy day?"

"Very much. We've been busy since opening our doors three months ago."

"Mostly cheating spouses and runaway teens, but I'll take it."

She frowned. "We can always ask the local police department if they need help on any cold cases."

"I might have to if I don't want to die from boredom." His grin widened. "Though I have to admit, even the cheating spouse cases have been more interesting than I expected. Last week's surveillance turned into quite the adventure when the husband's 'fishing trip' led us to that casino in Louisiana."

Pressley laughed, remembering how they'd spent two days tracking a man who claimed to be catching bass but was playing cards at the blackjack table. "At least his wife was relieved to find out he had a gambling problem instead of there being another woman. Easier to work through than infidelity."

"True. And the Wilson kid we found last month turned out to be camping in the national forest because he was afraid to tell his parents he'd been suspended from school." Jackson stretched back in his chair. "Sometimes the simple explanations are the right ones."

"And sometimes they're not." Pressley took another sip of her coffee, savoring the warmth. The late spring rain had brought an unexpected chill to the air, and she'd forgotten how quickly the weather could change in Arkansas. "Remember that missing person case from Magnolia? Everyone assumed the woman had left her husband, but—"

A young man burst through the door right before closing time. "I need help."

Jackson bolted to his feet. "Is someone after you?"

"No." His eyes darted from Jackson to Pressley and back. "My brother is missing."

"Please. Have a seat." Pressley motioned to the chair across from her. "How long has he been missing?"

"Two weeks." He sat and accepted the bottle of water Jackson offered. "He never came home from the prom. My parents are in Europe and will be home the day after tomorrow. I'd hoped that Ethan would come home before they did."

Pressley studied the young man's face. Dark circles under his eyes suggested he hadn't been sleeping well, and the way his hands shook slightly as he took the water bottle indicated he was more rattled than he was letting on. She'd seen that look before—the desperate hope mixed with growing dread that something terrible had happened.

"What's your name, son?" Jackson perched on the corner of Pressley's desk.

"Nate Duvall. I'm supposed to have watched out for Ethan." He pulled a phone from his pocket. "I got a text the night of the prom saying that my brother would be home late because he had to give a girl a ride."

"Did he say which girl?" Pressley asked.

Nate shook his head. "I've already asked the girl he went to the prom with. She hadn't seen him since she left the prom with another guy."

"Which direction would your brother have taken on his way home?"

"Highway 365. There aren't many houses on that road other than ours. I've already knocked on every door. No one claims to have seen my brother." Worry creased his brow as he showed them a photo of his brother.

Pressley examined the image on the phone screen. Ethan looked younger than his brother, with the same dark hair but a softer face. There was something earnest about his expression in the photo, the kind of kid who probably helped elderly neighbors with their groceries and never forgot his mother's birthday.

"May I send that to my email so I can print it off?" Jackson held out his hand.

Nate dropped the phone into his palm. "Ethan is a good kid. He wouldn't have taken off. The police don't seem to be too worried, but I am."

"What did the police say exactly?" Pressley leaned forward. She knew most of the officers in the county, and while they were generally competent, small-town departments sometimes lacked the resources for thorough missing person investigations.

"They filed a report, but they think he just ran off. Said eighteen-year-olds do it all the time." Nate's voice carried a bitter edge. "They don't know Ethan. He's been talking about college in the fall, about studying engineering at Arkansas Tech. He was excited about his future."

"What about your parents? When did you last speak to them?"

"This morning. They're cutting their trip short and flying back tomorrow instead of next week." Nate ran a hand through his hair. "Dad was furious that I waited so long to call them, but I kept thinking Ethan would show up. I didn't want to ruin their anniversary trip over nothing."

Pressley couldn't help but wonder how a man in his early twenties would be able to afford their fee. As if he read her mind, he said, "My parents will pay the cost. I told them about Ethan this morning. Like I said, they're pretty upset that I didn't say anything sooner."

As would any parent. "With any luck, we'll find your brother safe and sound before they return home." Pressley pulled a contract from her desk drawer. "Fill this out. We'll waive the retaining fee until your parents return."

"You'll start looking right away?"

"Absolutely." She glanced at Jackson, who nodded. "May I see the text?"

He handed her the phone. The message was short and typical of a teenager: "Giving a girl a ride home. Be back late. Don't wait up." After reading it, she returned the phone. "He didn't give much information."

"No, he didn't." Nate sighed and slid the phone back into his pocket. "He wouldn't lie, so I know there's a girl involved somehow. But none of his friends know anything about who it might have been."

"You've talked to his other friends?"

"Everyone I could think of. Ethan wasn't exactly popular, but he had a small group of guys he hung out with. They all said the same thing—that he seemed normal at the prom, maybe a little disappointed that

Jessica ditched him, but not upset enough to do anything crazy."

"His vehicle?"

Nate's shoulders slumped further. "I found it on the side of the road near an old farmhouse. Nothing inside but his tuxedo jacket."

"We'll need to take a look." Pressley pushed to her feet. "Mind if we follow you?"

The rain had let up when they followed the young man outside. Gray clouds still hung low over the town, and the air smelled of wet pavement and blooming dogwood trees. Nate climbed into a truck while they got into her Jeep.

"What's your take on this?" Jackson turned the key in the ignition.

"Two weeks is a long time for someone to stay away from home unless something happened." She clicked her seatbelt into place. "This girl, whoever she is, is the key. If we find her, we find out what happened that night."

"Could be as simple as he met someone and decided to extend his night. Maybe they've been holed up somewhere together."

"For two weeks? Without contacting his brother or returning his parents' calls?" Pressley shook her head. "No, something's not right here. And did you notice how nervous Nate got when I asked about the police? I think there's more to this story."

They followed Nate's taillights through the

winding country roads, past farmhouses and cattle pastures that looked almost ethereal in the misty evening light. The Duvall property was well-maintained, with fresh paint on the fence posts and neat flower beds flanking the driveway. Clearly a family that took pride in their home.

They followed Nate to his two-story house set away from the highway. Nate parked in front of a barn and led them inside to where an older model truck was parked. "This is my brother's. The jacket is still inside. Since I don't have the rest of the tux, I went ahead and purchased it from the shop."

"Ethan never went back?" Pressley pulled on a set of gloves and opened the driver's side door.

"No."

Not that she'd expected him to with his jacket draped over the passenger seat. The truck's interior was clean except for a few fast-food wrappers in the cup holder and a small stack of CDs on the dashboard. Classic rock mostly, with one country album mixed in. "We'll need to send the jacket in to forensics. See if they can find any DNA on the girl he picked up. Where, exactly, did you find his truck?"

"Three miles down from here. There's a dirt road that leads to the south. An old woman lives down that road, but all she did was mumble something about a dead girl."

Pressley met Jackson's gaze through the truck's interior. "Guess we need to talk to this woman." She straightened and faced Nate. "Did your brother own a laptop? If so, may we see it?"

"Sure. It's in his room." Nate watched as Jackson bagged the tuxedo jacket, then led them into the house.

Pressley glanced around the neat entryway and into each room they passed on the way to the stairs. Cleaner than she'd expected with two young men living alone for a while. Family photos covered the walls—graduation pictures, vacation shots, what looked like a recent family portrait taken at a professional studio. The Duvalls appeared to be a close-knit family, which made Ethan's disappearance even more puzzling.

Then, they entered Ethan's room.

A typical teenage boy's room. Posters of bands and girls in bikinis, a gaming console hooked up to a flat screen TV, dirty clothes on the floor, an unmade bed, and a desk cluttered with notebooks and a laptop. But there were also signs of a more serious side—college brochures stacked neatly on the nightstand, a calendar with important dates marked in careful handwriting, textbooks that looked like they'd been read.

Nate opened the laptop and typed in the password. "I cracked it a long time ago." A weak grin spread across his face. "Brothers, you know?"

While Jackson roamed around the room, examining the contents of the dresser and closet, Pressley searched Ethan's social media page and folders. His Facebook page showed typical teenage posts—complaints about homework, excitement about the prom, jokes shared with friends. Nothing to give any indication about why an otherwise happy young man would run off. His browser history was equally unremarkable: YouTube videos, news sites, college websites, and a few searches about Arkansas Tech's engineering program.

"Do you have the name and address of his prom date?"

"Jessica Murphy." Nate's brow furrowed. "She lives in town. Second Avenue, I think. I don't really know her since she's my brother's age."

Jackson typed into his phone. "I found a Murphy on Second Avenue. Want to stop by there on the way home? We can visit the older woman tomorrow. Folks around here don't like to be disturbed at suppertime."

Nodding, Pressley chuckled. "Heaven forbid we disrupt supper." She clapped a hand on Nate's shoulder. "Call us any time with an update. We'll find your brother." Alive or dead.

Back in town, Jackson rang the doorbell on the house with Murphy painted on the mailbox. The house was a well-kept Victorian with a wraparound porch and flower boxes under every window. Wind chimes tinkled softly in the evening breeze, and warm light spilled from the front windows, giving the whole scene a cozy, welcoming feel.

A woman in her forties answered, drying her hand on a dishtowel. "May I help you?"

"We're investigators Hudson and Taylor," Jackson

said, showing his ID. "We'd like to speak to Jessica about Ethan Duvall. He's missing, and we found out they went to prom together."

Her eyes widened. "Oh, my goodness, missing? Sure, but they didn't leave the prom together. Jessica!" She motioned to a sofa. "She'll be right down."

"Thank you." Pressley smiled and took a seat, glancing around the tastefully decorated room. Family photos lined the fireplace mantel. Jessica appeared to be an only child, judging by the progression of school photos and family portraits spanning what looked like eighteen years.

"You wanted to see me?" A pretty blond girl with big blue eyes joined them. She was still wearing her cheerleading warm-up suit, and her hair was pulled back in a high ponytail. Even without makeup, she was striking. The kind of girl who'd never lacked for attention.

"No need to be afraid." Pressley pasted on what she hoped was a welcoming smile. "You went to prom with Ethan Duvall?"

She nodded and sat in a winged chair. "Yes, but I left with someone else."

"We heard. May I ask why?"

She sighed, looking suddenly younger and less confident. "Ethan was nice and all. Too nice, actually. Kind of boring. He wanted us to go out."

"Steady?"

"Yes, but I don't want to. I'm head cheerleader and

can have my pick of any of the guys." The words came out automatically, like something she'd said many times before, but there was a hint of uncertainty in her voice.

Pressley fought the urge to roll her eyes. "Who did you leave with?" Head football player if she hazarded a guess.

"Billy Wilson. The quarterback."

Of course. "Are you aware that no one has seen Ethan in two weeks?"

She nodded, twisting her hands in her lap. "His brother told me. That isn't like Ethan. He's never in trouble. He's one of the smartest guys in our class. He was supposed to give the valedictorian speech at graduation next month."

That was new information. "He picked up a girl on the highway and gave her a ride home. Any idea who that might be?"

Her eyes widened. "None of our schoolmates live out that way except him and his brother, but…"

"But what?" Pressley leaned closer.

"There are stories around this time every year."

"What kind of stories?" Jackson asked.

"It's just an urban legend. No one really believes the stories, except…" She took a deep, shuddering breath. "A guy disappears every year at prom time."

The room fell silent except for the ticking of an antique clock on the mantel. Jessica's mother appeared in the doorway, concern etched on her face.

"What kind of urban legend?" Pressley kept her

voice gentle, but she could feel her pulse quickening. This was the kind of detail that could change everything.

Chapter Two

The heck with it being suppertime. Pressley couldn't resist questioning the old woman on Highway 365 after Jessica's statement. The disappearance of Ethan Duvall had just gotten weirder. They definitely had a mystery on their hands.

"You sure about this?" Jackson asked as they drove through the gathering dusk. "People around here take their evening routines seriously."

"After what Jessica just told us, I'm not waiting until tomorrow." Pressley gripped the steering wheel tighter. "If there's some kind of pattern to these disappearances, we need to know now."

The evening light cast long shadows as Pressley and Jackson pulled up to the farmhouse. The property felt untouched by the rush of modern life, as if time had stopped somewhere in the 1950s. Paint peeled from the shutters, and weeds grew tall around the foundation, yet the structure remained solid and imposing against the darkening sky. A rusty mailbox leaned at an odd angle, the name "Hensley" barely visible through years of weather damage.

The porch creaked under their steps as they approached the front door. Pressley noticed several wind chimes hanging from the eaves, their melodic tinkling the only sound in the stillness. A pair of rocking chairs sat motionless, as if their occupants had just stepped inside.

Jackson gave a one-knuckle knock. An old woman, blue eyes as sharp as a tack in a weathered face, peered at them through the window. Her silver hair was pulled back in a neat bun, and despite her advanced age, her gaze held an intensity that made Pressley shift uncomfortably.

"What do you want?" The voice was clear and strong, carrying none of the frailty one might expect from someone who appeared to be in her eighties.

Pressley held her identification up to the glass. "We have a few questions about a missing young man who we believe might have stopped by here."

A curtain fell into place seconds before the door opened. "A couple of young men have been by. Come in. I've coffee on. My name is Mildred Hensley."

They stepped into a living room that seemed frozen in another era. The furniture was well-maintained but clearly decades old. A burgundy velvet sofa with wooden legs, doilies on every surface, and a grandfather clock ticking rhythmically in the corner.

The room smelled faintly of lavender and old books. The walls were adorned with sepia-toned photographs in ornate frames. A wood-burning stove radiated too much warmth for the mild evening. Pressley coughed against the woody smell and the sudden stuffiness.

"Sit. I'll be right back." Mrs. Hensley bustled through an archway into a kitchen, her movements surprisingly spry for her age.

Pressley stepped in front of the photos while Jackson examined the room's other details. Several showed a younger Mrs. Hensley with a girl who could only be her twin. Both had the same striking eyes and delicate features. Two lovely girls, their smiles frozen in time, wearing the fashions of the 1940s. A few others showed an older couple, obviously the parents, standing proudly beside their daughters. Something was haunting about the images, perhaps because Pressley now knew one of those bright-eyed girls had met such a tragic end.

"Beautiful family," Jackson murmured, joining her.

"Here we go. There are sugar and cream if you like." Mrs. Hensley set a silver tray on the coffee table. The service was elegant—fine china cups with delicate rose patterns, matching cream and sugar bowls, and small silver spoons. "Now, how can I help you?"

Jackson showed a photo of Ethan. "Have you seen this young man?"

Mrs. Hensley studied the image carefully,

adjusting a pair of reading glasses that hung from a chain around her neck. "He came by two weeks ago looking for Lilly." She poured coffee into three mugs with practiced precision.

"Who is Lilly?" Pressley accepted a mug and added a generous amount of cream and a bit of sugar while Jackson took his black. The coffee was stronger than she preferred, with a bitter aftertaste that made her grimace slightly.

"My sister." The woman sat in a rocking chair across from the sofa, the chair creaking softly as she settled. "The young man said he gave her a ride, lent her his jacket, but that's impossible. Lilly died back in the forties."

Pressley frowned, setting down her cup. "Any idea who he might have given a ride to?"

"Not many girls go walking down this road alone at night. Another young man came by looking for the first one—must have been his brother. I told him the same thing I'm telling you. The young man you're looking for isn't the first to say he gave my sister a ride. It's been going on since I was sixteen." Mrs. Hensley's voice carried a matter-of-fact tone, as if she were discussing the weather rather than decades of mysterious encounters.

Pressley exchanged a look with Jackson. Since she didn't believe in ghosts, someone had to be pretending to be Lilly. The question was why. "Has anyone ever reported these incidents to the police?"

"Oh, some have tried over the years. But what's to report? A young man claims he picked up a girl, gave her his coat, and then couldn't find her the next day. Police have better things to do than chase ghost stories." Mrs. Hensley rocked gently, her expression unreadable.

"My sister's grave is out back if you want to take a look." Mrs. Hensley tilted her head toward the rear of the house. "As far as I know, the missing young man headed that way. Could be that he got lost in the woods. If so, he's a goner by now. Lots of bears up this way." Her eyes twinkled in contrast with the seriousness of the situation.

"May I ask how your sister died?" Jackson asked, his voice gentle but persistent.

The woman's friendliness turned to ice. Her rocking stopped abruptly, and the temperature in the room seemed to drop several degrees. "She was assaulted, killed, and dumped in a ditch on prom night." She turned back to Pressley, seeming to prefer talking to her rather than Jackson. "Sixteen years old. Just a child, really. Had her whole life ahead of her."

"Why would someone pretend to be her?" Pressley shifted uncomfortably on the plaid sofa, the horsehair stuffing prickling through the worn fabric.

Mrs. Hensley shrugged, resuming her gentle rocking. "Lots of folks say her spirit haunts this highway every year on prom night. Some young man sees her and decides to act chivalrous by offering her a ride. My sister was very pretty, you know. No man could resist her charms. They'd give her their coat, then come back for it the next day only to find out it couldn't possibly have been Lilly they gave a ride to. Ghosts don't exist, now do they?" She smiled, but the expression didn't reach her eyes.

"No, ma'am, they don't." Pressley got to her feet without taking a sip of her coffee. The bitter taste still lingered on her tongue. "We'll head to the grave if you don't mind." She dropped a business card onto the tray. "Please give us a call if you have any information for us."

"I'll do that," Mrs. Hensley said, though her tone suggested otherwise.

Outside, away from the house, Pressley felt like she could breathe again. The evening air was cool and fresh compared to the stifling atmosphere inside. She turned to Jackson, who was loosening his collar.

"I don't creep out easily, but that old woman creeps me out. She's hiding something."

"And clearly doesn't like men." He put a hand on the small of her back as they headed toward the rear of the property. "Did you notice how she warmed up when she was talking to you but turned cold when I asked about her sister's death?"

The graveyard was small and overgrown, surrounded by a wrought-iron fence that had seen better days. Moss covered many of the older headstones, and ivy crept up the fence posts. It was the kind of place that would be beautiful in daylight but felt ominous in the gathering darkness.

"Look." Jackson pointed out footprints too large to be a woman's pressed into the soft earth near one particular grave. "It hasn't rained since the night of the prom. Looks like Ethan might've been here."

"At least someone was." She read the name on the marble tombstone, which was newer and better maintained than the others. Lilly Hensley, 1930-1946. "Beloved daughter and sister." Fresh flowers lay at the base—white roses that couldn't have been there more than a few days.

Pressley knelt and examined the flowers more closely. "These are recent. Someone's been taking care of this grave."

"Mrs. Hensley?"

"Maybe. Or maybe whoever's been impersonating Lilly." She stood and faced the woods that bordered the property. The trees seemed to stretch endlessly into darkness, and she could hear the distant sound of an owl calling. Time to let the local police know there might be a body somewhere out there. She hoped to find Ethan alive, but with the passage of time, it wasn't looking realistic. "Let's head back. I want to see how long this Lilly thing has really been going on. See whether we can find any details about her death."

"You thinking what I'm thinking?" Jackson asked as they walked back toward their vehicle.

"That someone's been using this ghost story to

cover up murders for decades? Yeah, I'm thinking exactly that."

They worked late into the night after letting the police department know that Ethan might've wandered into the woods looking for Lilly. The police had been skeptical but agreed to organize a search party for the following morning. Back at the office, everything they could find, dating back to May 25th, 1946, the evening of Lilly's death, lay spread out on a table in front of them.

The original police report made for grim reading. The girl had been brutally raped, then strangled, and found the next morning lying in a ditch less than a mile from her home. She'd been wearing a pale blue dress, her prom dress, and one white high-heeled shoe. The other shoe was never found. Her attacker had never been identified, let alone caught. Some speculated a returning soldier or transient passing through had happened upon her walking home and leaped at the chance to assault a young woman alone.

Jackson had arranged newspaper articles by date, creating a timeline that stretched across seven decades. "These are the papers that mention any missing young men around prom time."

"This has been going on for a long time." Pressley rubbed her tired eyes. The office felt too quiet, with only the hum of the coffee maker and the occasional car passing on the street below.

He nodded. "Makes you kind of wonder whether

ghosts are real, doesn't it?"

"No. There's always an explanation." She picked up the first paper and scanned it, adjusting the desk lamp for better light. "In 1947 a soldier home from the war disappeared. Robert Mitchell, twenty-two years old. His car was found on Highway 365 with the engine still running. In 1956, a farmer's son swore he saw a girl walking barefoot along the road, but he didn't stop. Another young man disappeared that night. David Crawford, age nineteen. His body was never found."

She continued reading, her voice growing more troubled with each account. "In 1978, two young men from Memphis claimed to have picked up Lilly. One of the men never made it home. The other said he'd dropped his friend and Lilly off at the address she'd given, but when he returned the next day, there was no sign of either of them. The survivor, Marcus Thompson, was so traumatized he spent three months in a psychiatric facility."

"Man," Jackson muttered. "How did we never hear about this pattern before?"

"Because people don't want to believe it." She glanced at Jackson, then picked up the next article. "In 1993, a local reporter covering urban legends interviewed several witnesses who had heard of other incidents that didn't make it into the papers." The reporter, Sarah Gordon, had been investigating for a book about Arkansas folklore when she stumbled onto what she believed was a genuine mystery. Her notes, included in the file Jackson had compiled, suggested she'd interviewed at least a dozen people with stories about the Highway 365 ghost.

"How many disappearances went unreported?" Pressley wondered aloud. Several years' worth, if the rumors of one a year during prom time were correct.

"In 2005, a trucker's dashcam captured what appeared to be a young woman near a bend on Arkansas 365. Being behind schedule, he didn't stop, but when he drove by the next day and pulled over out of curiosity, he spotted a single white rose lying near the ditch—the same spot where Lilly's body was found." The trucker, James Morrison, had turned the footage over to police, but the image quality was too poor to make out any details about the figure.

"In 2014, a college student blogging about urban legends recounted her boyfriend's disappearance after dropping her at home. In 2023, someone disappeared. A sketch of a girl looking exactly like Lilly Hensley was found on the passenger seat of his vehicle." Pressley set down the last article and stretched her aching back. "Any ideas?"

"Nope. None of it makes sense." He plopped into a chair, the leather creaking under his weight. "I did find the name of a young man who was the primary suspect in Lilly's death. Tommy Raney, a local boy. History of violence against women. The police never could prove anything because he disappeared a week after Lilly's murder."

"Convenient timing."

"Very. His disappearance was what started the whole ghost legend. People said Lilly's spirit had taken her revenge."

"What if this Lilly is still alive, exacting her revenge? Or someone else wants revenge for her death" Pressley stacked the papers back in order, her mind racing through possibilities.

"She'd be the same age as Mildred. I don't see anyone mistaking an old woman for a teenage girl, no matter how good her genes are."

"No, but there could be family members willing to help. Daughters, granddaughters, nieces. I know it's a long shot, but maybe Lilly's family is out for revenge by killing any young man unknowingly reenacting the events of the night Lilly was murdered."

"Definitely a long shot." He rubbed his hands roughly down his face. "It's late. We might think more clearly after a few hours of sleep."

"Because this happened so long ago—" Pressley said, fighting back a yawn, "there aren't any witnesses other than Mildred to question. Anyone else will only repeat the legend without giving us anything concrete to go on."

"We figured out who The Phantom from 1946 was, so we'll get to the bottom of this one, too." Jackson stood and stretched, his joints popping audibly. "Besides, Ethan might still be alive out there. We can't give up on him."

Sleep didn't come until two a.m., and even then, it was fitful. Pressley dreamed of a pale girl in a blue dress walking endlessly along a dark highway, her face always just out of view. At seven, she groaned and threw aside the blankets on her bed and padded to the kitchen in her apartment over the office of Hudson and Taylor. The morning light streaming through her windows felt like a blessing after the dark dreams.

By the time she had coffee going, Jackson strolled through her door with a box in his hands and his hair still damp from a shower.

"Good morning." He placed a tender kiss on her neck. "Sleep okay?"

"Not really. You?" She leaned into his warmth, grateful for his solid presence after the night's unsettling dreams.

"Nope." He grinned. "Dreamed of pretty, dark-haired ghosts. And bears. Lots of bears."

"Any clues in those dreams?" She handed him a cup, noting the dark circles under his eyes that matched her own.

"Someone is luring young men to their deaths, and it's been happening for a very long time. The question is whether we're dealing with one very old, very clever killer, or a family tradition."

"Ready to think revenge?"

"Yep. I definitely think we have a serial killer on our hands. Probably more than one, given the timeline."

"I've never heard of generational serial killers."

"Me neither, but there's always a first time." He set the box on the table. "Doughnuts. Figured we'd need the sugar today."

The phone rang downstairs, shrill and insistent in the morning quiet.

"I'm sorry. I forgot to forward calls to my cell." Pressley moved toward the door.

"I'll get it." Jackson rushed downstairs, taking the steps two at a time. He returned a couple of minutes later, his expression grim. "Police are heading over to Highway 365 around nine and said we could join them. They found something."

"What kind of something?" Pressley felt her stomach clench.

"Clothing. In the woods behind the Hensley place. They think it might be Ethan's."

"Great. Maybe between all of us, we'll uncover something." Maybe even dig up a living, breathing ghost. But as Pressley looked at Jackson's serious expression, she had a sinking feeling that whatever they found in those woods wouldn't be good news for Ethan Duvall.

Chapter Three

Pressley and Jackson, along with a slew of law enforcement officers, gathered on the stretch of road passing Mrs. Hensley's place. The morning air carried a chill that seemed to seep into everyone's bones, and the overcast sky promised rain before the day was through. The ditches on either side of the road sported knee-high weeds that led to dense forest. Yellow crime scene tape fluttered in the breeze, marking off areas already deemed significant. Digging equipment waited to be used. Shovels, metal detectors, and even a small excavator that had been brought in on a flatbed truck.

The detective in charge, one Leon Anderson, whistled to get everyone's attention. He was a tall, weathered man in his fifties with graying hair and the kind of steady demeanor that came from decades of dealing with the worst humanity had to offer. "We'll let the cadaver dogs sniff around first, then start digging if they target anything. I want whatever is found to be placed on that blue tarp over there." He pointed to a large tarpaulin spread on the ground. "If it's a body, place it on the black tarp, and the medical examiner will take over from there."

So, he felt the same as Pressley. He didn't expect to find Ethan alive. The grim reality of the situation settled over the assembled group like a heavy blanket.

Mrs. Hensley marched down the dirt road that led to her house and watched from a distance, her face wearing a scowl that could have curdled milk. She didn't look pleased to have them there, which was understandable given the circumstances, but something in her expression went beyond normal irritation. If she was unhappy about their presence on the roadside, she wouldn't appreciate them digging on her property.

The cadaver dogs, two German Shepherds with their handlers, were released and searched the area methodically, noses to the ground. Their training was evident in their focused movements as they quartered the area in precise patterns. Pressley watched their behavior closely, knowing that these animals could detect the scent of decomposition even when buried several feet underground.

"I found my brother's truck there." Nate Duvall pointed to a tree that had been struck by lightning at some point in the past, its blackened trunk a stark reminder of nature's power. "On the road, though. Not in the ditch."

Pressley followed Jackson to the spot, her boots crunching on the gravel shoulder. No sign remained that any vehicle had been parked there. No tire tracks, no oil stains, nothing to indicate a car had sat abandoned for two weeks. But she placed an evidence identification marker on the road anyway. They couldn't leave any stone unturned. Not if they wanted to find out what had been happening here since the mid-1940s.

Two men with shovels started digging in an area just off the road that dipped lower than the surrounding area and looked recently disturbed. The soil was softer here, easier to work with, suggesting it had been turned over not too long ago. The rhythmic sound of metal biting into earth created an ominous soundtrack to their investigation.

It didn't take long to uncover a browning carnation, the kind that would adorn the lapel of a tuxedo. The once-white petals had turned the color of old parchment, and the stem was brittle with age.

"My brother wore a white carnation to the prom." Nate stared into the hole, his face pale with recognition. "Why would it be buried?"

"Looks like a place for souvenirs." Jackson hunkered down beside the hole, careful not to contaminate the scene. "Here's the right shoe of a pair of black Nikes. Size eleven, from the looks of it."

The more the diggers uncovered, the more Pressley felt as if she were stepping back in time. Vintage shoe styles from different decades—oxfords from the fifties, loafers from the seventies, athletic shoes from the nineties. Old-fashioned eyeglass styles with thick frames and wire rims. The tattered remnant of a once frilly shawl that might have been fashionable in the sixties. A class ring from 1987. A watch that had stopped working long ago. "Why would someone keep these things?"

"A lot of serial killers keep mementos," Jackson said, standing and brushing dirt from his knees. "Trophies to help them relive their crimes."

"You still think we're dealing with a serial killer?"

He nodded grimly. "More than one. Has to be, given the timeline. At least that's the angle I'm going to work unless we find out otherwise."

Pressley would follow his lead. At least he had a theory to work with. The whole situation left her feeling like she was trying to solve a puzzle with half the pieces missing.

The pile on the blue tarp grew steadily. Each item told a story of a young life cut short, dreams that would never be fulfilled. The shovel in one man's hands clinked against something metallic buried deeper than the other artifacts. The man bent and retrieved a metal box, its surface green with oxidation, which he handed to Pressley with gloved hands.

Pressley opened the lid with careful fingers and stared at dozens of black and white photos of young men dating back as far as the disappearances. Some were formal portraits, others candid shots that looked like they'd been taken without the subjects' knowledge. The photos were arranged chronologically, creating a horrifying timeline of victims. Definitely keepsakes of a deranged mind. She glanced at Mrs. Hensley, who stood about fifty feet away, plucking nervously at the fringe on her shawl. "I think I'll see if she recognizes any of these men." She carried the box carefully across the uneven ground.

"Mrs. Hensley—"

"Not Mrs. I never married." The correction came sharp and quick, as if she'd had to make it many times before.

"My apologies. Do you recognize this box?" Pressley held it out, watching the woman's face for any telltale reaction.

"Nope." But her eyes had flickered to the box and away again, just for a split second.

"Are you sure?" She opened the lid, angling it so the woman could see the contents. "Know any of these young men?"

Miss Hensley leaned forward slightly, and Pressley caught a whiff of lavender water and something else— something medicinal. "The one on top is the boy you're looking for."

"Yes, ma'am." Pressley kept her gaze fixed on the woman's face, looking for any crack in her composed facade. A flicker of something she couldn't identify…satisfaction? regret? fear?—crossed her features before the woman turned her attention back to the digging.

"When are they going to start tearing up my property?" The question held an edge of anxiety that hadn't been there before.

"They won't unless the dogs smell something that could be a dead body."

"Good." She turned back toward the house, but her steps were slower than before, less certain.

"We'll be searching the area around your sister's grave."

That stopped her in her tracks. Eyes narrowed to slits, she whirled to face Pressley with surprising agility for a woman her age. "I will not allow you to desecrate my sister's resting place."

"I assure you we will treat her grave with the utmost respect." Pressley kept her voice calm and professional, but she could feel the tension radiating from the older woman.

"Hmmph." Miss Hensley marched down the dirt road, her back rigid with indignation.

Pressley returned to Jackson's side, still holding the metal box. "I still think she's withholding information. Did you see how she reacted when I mentioned searching near her sister's grave?"

"We'll find out the truth." He grinned, but it didn't reach his eyes. "You're great at digging up secrets."

"I dug up one." Her face flushed at his praise. Finding the identity of The Phantom would always be one of her greatest achievements, the case that had established their reputation and brought them to Arkansas in the first place.

A tow truck rumbled to a stop a few feet away, its diesel engine coughing before falling silent. A man in denim coveralls climbed out and approached them, his weathered face curious but cautious. "You still looking for that Duvall kid?"

"Yes, sir." Jackson faced the man, noting the company logo on his shirt—Murphy's Towing, established 1978.

"Name's Bill Murphy. I drove by here the night he went missing, saw his empty vehicle. Waited a few minutes in case he'd gone into the woods to take care of business, you know? But I never did see him. There isn't usually a lot of traffic on this highway, especially that late."

"May I ask your purpose for being here that night?" Pressley tilted her head, genuinely curious.

"Work. Had to pull a tractor out of a mudhole about five miles down the road. Farmer called around midnight, said his equipment was stuck good and tight." He gestured vaguely southward. "Took me near three hours to get it out."

"Do you know the woman who lives down that road?" She jerked her head in the direction of the Hensley home.

"Mildred. No one knows her very well. She's a recluse, always has been since I was a kid. Only goes into town once a week for groceries and the occasional doctor's appointment. She isn't what we'd call friendly. Talks to herself more than she talks to other people."

"Have you heard what happened to her sister?"

"Sure." He crossed his arms, leaning against the side of his truck. "Everyone around here grew up on that story and the rumors that her ghost haunts this road every May. Course, most folks think it's just nonsense. You won't see hide nor hair of any ghost again until next year's prom."

"Do you believe the story?"

He laughed, but it was a nervous sound. "Nah. It's just something to make kids behave during prom season. Like the boogeyman. Though I'll admit, this stretch of road always gave me the creeps, even as a kid."

"You've never seen the ghost?" Jackson arched a brow.

"Nope. But then again, I didn't come down this road the night of my prom. Had better sense than that." He glanced around at the assembled law enforcement. "Looks like you folks found more than you bargained for."

"Thank you for your time." Pressley set the metal box carefully on the blue tarp with the other evidence. The man hadn't told them anything they didn't already know, but every piece of information helped build the bigger picture.

Something rustled in the trees beyond the crime

scene tape, drawing her attention. Pressley strained her eyes to see what could've made the sound. At first, she thought maybe a squirrel had run up a tree, but the sound came again—deliberate, purposeful—this time attracting Jackson's attention as well.

"Let's check it out." He thanked the tow truck driver, who climbed back into his vehicle and drove away with a final curious glance. Jackson then led Pressley toward the tree line, both of them instinctively checking their weapons.

The sounds of digging and conversations among law enforcement faded the further they went into the woods. Their feet crunched on dried leaves fallen during the previous autumn, and somewhere overhead, a woodpecker hammered against dead bark. The forest was dense here, with towering oaks and maples creating a canopy that blocked most of the overcast sky. A squirrel chattered its displeasure at their intrusion, but the sound they'd heard was definitely not wildlife.

Something white moved in and out of the shadows ahead, appearing and disappearing like a will-o'-the-wisp. "Looks like our ghost," Jackson said quietly, pulling his weapon from its holster but keeping it pointed toward the ground.

"A ghost wouldn't run from us." More movement to her right had Pressley drawing her gun as well. The white shapes seemed to be leading them deeper into the forest, always staying just out of clear view. "Think we've got more than one." She stepped closer to

Jackson's side, counting at least three figures in what appeared to be white dresses or robes.

A high-pitched giggle came from behind them, sending chills down Pressley's spine. She whipped around, scanning the shadows between the trees. She still couldn't get a good look at whoever was toying with them. The figures seemed to know the woods intimately, moving through areas where the underbrush was thickest, using the trees as cover. "We should head back. We're being led farther away from the others." She was a journalist turned private investigator, not a police officer trained for tactical situations in unfamiliar terrain.

"You're right." Jackson put his weapon away and took her hand. His palm was warm and steady, grounding her. "We'll return with backup and proper equipment."

When they rejoined the main group, the atmosphere had grown more tense. The cadaver dogs had become increasingly agitated, their handlers having to work harder to keep them focused.

Pressley led Detective Anderson and several officers to Lilly's grave. The dogs immediately went crazy, barking and pawing at the ground around the marble headstone. Their behavior was unmistakable. They'd found something significant.

"There are more here than just one body," the dogs' handler said grimly, his years of experience evident in his assessment. "We're looking at multiple bodies. This whole area is compromised."

Detective Anderson muttered a curse under his breath that would have made his mother wash his mouth out with soap. "Someone fetch the old woman. If there are bodies buried here, she has to have known about them. You can't dig graves this close to someone's house without them noticing."

Miss Hensley, scowl in place and looking every bit like an angry schoolmarm, disagreed vehemently and pointed to her hearing aids. "I take these out at night. I can't hear anything when I do. Do not disturb that grave!" She stomped toward a man with a shovel, moving with surprising speed for someone her age.

"Ma'am." Anderson stopped her with a gentle but firm hand on her arm. "Do not hinder our investigation. We will have to search this grave and dig up the surrounding area. Would you like one of my officers to bring you a seat? You can supervise to make sure nothing happens to the remains of your sister." He then went on to mumble about it being against the law to bury human bodies on private property without proper permits and health department approval.

"Got a relatively fresh one, Detective." An officer waved Anderson over to a spot about ten feet from Lilly's headstone.

Pressley and Jackson followed, their footsteps muffled by the soft earth. She stared at the uncovered hand, pale and waxy in death. The cuff of a white shirt peeked out from the soil, and she could see what looked like the edge of a black bow tie. Had they found Ethan?

"I have no idea how he got there." Miss Hensley plopped onto a folding lawn chair that one of the officers had retrieved from a patrol car. "Someone is messing with my land. Probably kids playing pranks."

"By burying dead people?" Pressley shook her head in disbelief. Her gut told her the woman was neck deep in whatever was happening here, and she wouldn't stop until she proved her theory correct. A ninety-something woman might not be able to commit the murders physically, but she had a hand in orchestrating them.

"It is certainly turning into quite a graveyard," Miss Hensley observed with what sounded almost like pride.

Pressley rolled her eyes and watched as the rest of Ethan's body was carefully uncovered. He lay in a shallow grave, his formal wear now stained with earth and decay. His features were almost unrecognizable from the beating he'd taken—his face swollen and discolored, his nose broken. Someone had inflicted a tremendous amount of violence on this young man before killing him.

His brother Nate cried out and fell to his knees, covering his face with his hands. "I didn't think he'd really be dead. I kept hoping..." His voice broke, and the sound of his grief cut through the professional atmosphere like a knife.

"Are you making a positive ID that this is your

brother?" Anderson asked gently, his voice surprisingly tender for such a gruff man.

"It's him. See the birthmark behind his ear?" Nate's voice was barely a whisper.

Pressley craned her neck to see a red mark shaped remarkably like the boot of Italy, just as Nate had described. She sighed and stepped out of the way as the body was carefully removed and placed in a body bag. She put an arm around Nate's shoulders and helped him to his feet. "Come on. Let these people do their work."

"My parents are going to be devastated. They're supposed to land in Little Rock in three hours." He wiped his nose with the back of his hand, looking suddenly much younger than his twenty-something years.

"We'll let them know that we will do everything in our power to find those responsible for this."

"This is our investigation now, Miss Taylor," Anderson said firmly but not unkindly. "We'll handle things from here on out. I appreciate your help in locating the victim, but this is now a homicide investigation."

Once they were out of earshot of the detective, she reassured the young man that she and Jackson would continue to investigate what happened to Ethan, regardless of official jurisdiction. "You're paying us to do a job, and we'll get it done. We don't stop just because the police take over."

He nodded gratefully. "Thank you. I'm sure my

parents will want to talk to both of you when they get back. Can I go home? I really don't want to see my little brother in a body bag."

"Yes. We know where to find you if we need anything else."

Tears coursing down his face, he climbed into his truck with shaking hands and drove off, leaving tire tracks in the soft shoulder.

"I really hoped we'd find Ethan alive," Jackson said, watching the truck disappear around a bend.

"Me, too." Pressley's shoulders slumped with the weight of disappointment and growing dread. "Don't you find it strange that the mementos were kept so close to the victims?" Would they find all the other young men who had disappeared over the decades buried in this makeshift cemetery?

"If the old woman is involved, she'd want them kept close to her. She doesn't look like she has enough strength to dig graves, though. Someone's been helping her."

"No, the ghosts we saw in the woods helped her." Pressley glanced toward the tree line, half-expecting to catch another glimpse of white moving between the trees. "She'll crack eventually. No one can keep this kind of secret for as long as she has without making mistakes."

"No one would've known anything if Nate hadn't come to our office," Jackson pointed out. "We've already done our part in finding Ethan."

"There's a lot more to do. Those other families deserve answers too."

By the end of the day, more than fifteen bodies had been uncovered and loaded into the medical examiner's van for DNA testing and identification. The victims ranged in age from teenagers to young men in their twenties, and the condition of the remains suggested they'd been buried over a span of several decades. Such a waste of young lives, each representing shattered dreams and grieving families.

Pressley switched her gaze to Miss Hensley, who had spent the entire day knitting in her chair, occasionally glancing up as if watching a mildly interesting movie play out in front of her. Her composure was unnatural—most people would be horrified to discover a mass grave on their property, but she seemed almost entertained by the proceedings. What secret was she hiding? No way could a woman her age have given Ethan the vicious beating that killed him. Who and how many people were helping her carry out these murders?

"We need to find out whether she has family," Pressley said quietly. "I know she said she never married, but she's lying about something."

Jackson nodded grimly. "I agree. Everything that comes out of that woman's mouth is suspect. We just have to prove it, and we need to figure out who those people in white were. They're the key to all this."

Chapter Four

Pressley surveyed last night's scene in the morning light, noting how different everything looked without the chaos of the investigation. The crime scene tape still fluttered in the breeze, and deep gouges in the earth marked where the bodies had been unearthed. The normally peaceful countryside felt violated, scarred by the revelation of decades of violence. She then stepped onto the porch to question Mildred in more depth—this time without the company of local law enforcement. Since they'd been to her home a couple of times before, Pressley hoped the woman would be more trusting of them, though trust seemed like an unlikely commodity where Mildred Hensley was concerned.

The morning air carried the scent of honeysuckle and impending rain. Dark clouds gathered on the horizon, promising another stormy afternoon. The Hensley house looked different in daylight—less ominous but somehow more tragic, like a monument to lives that had been frozen in time by grief.

Mildred scowled when she opened the door in response to Jackson's polite knock. Her gray hair was perfectly arranged despite the early hour, and she wore a faded housedress that had probably been fashionable in the 1960s. "Guess I'd best put on some tea. As many times as the two of you come by, folks would think we were friends." She bustled into the kitchen, leaving them alone in the living room with its collection of memories and secrets.

Friends was the last thing they were, in Pressley's opinion. The woman had been evasive and hostile from their first meeting, and yesterday's discovery of multiple bodies had only reinforced Pressley's suspicion that Mildred knew far more than she was letting on. She moved to the mantel to study the family photographs in more detail, searching for clues she might have missed before.

The Hensleys had once been a happy family, but the photos told a story of gradual decline. The earlier pictures showed four people radiating joy and contentment. The parents were handsome and prosperous-looking, the twin daughters beautiful and full of life. But the later photos, the ones taken after Lilly's death, showed the survivors hollow-eyed and grim. They no longer smiled in the pictures without Lilly in them, as if her absence had drained all happiness from their world.

One thing stood out to Pressley more than any

other detail. In a family that documented every milestone and celebration, why wasn't there a photo of Lilly in a prom dress? Every other significant event in the girls' lives seemed to be represented, graduations, birthdays, church events, but nothing from what should have been one of the most important nights of a young woman's life.

"Here." Mildred set a tray of tea and cookies on the coffee table with more force than necessary, the china rattling ominously. She then plopped into her rocking chair, the springs creaking under her weight. "What do you want this time?"

Pressley poured the three of them cups of watered-down tea, bypassing the cookies that looked as hard as rocks and probably twice as old. The tea service was elegant but showed its age. Hairline cracks in the cups and worn spots on the silver spoons. "We'd like to hear more about Lilly. We realize we don't know much about her as a person."

"What kind of a person was she?" Jackson smiled encouragingly, using the gentle tone that had served him well during his police interrogations.

Mildred's eyes took on a faraway look, and for a moment, the harsh lines around her mouth softened. "She lit up a room with her smile. Innocent. Pure as snow, that girl. Everyone who met her loved her instantly." A sadness clouded the woman's eyes, the first genuine emotion Pressley had seen from her. "My family never recovered after her violent death. It broke us all, one by one."

Pressley took a sip of her tea and fought back a grimace at the bitterness of it. The liquid was pale and flavorless, as if Mildred had used the same tea leaves multiple times. "Why isn't there a picture of her in her prom dress? Most families would have dozens of photos from such an important night."

"I never said she went to the prom. Only that she was killed on prom night." Mildred hitched her chin defiantly, as if daring them to challenge her. "You assumed she went? Well, you know what they say about assuming."

The correction hit Pressley like a physical blow. In all their research and investigation, they'd somehow taken it for granted that Lilly had been returning from the prom when she was attacked. But if she hadn't attended, what had she been doing out on the highway that night?

"My apologies." Pressley glanced out the window, noting how the trees seemed to press closer to the house than they had the day before. "We saw something yesterday that confused us. It appeared as if several women in white dresses ran through the trees. Would you know anything about that?"

Mildred snorted, a sound that held no humor. "The woods go on for miles and miles. I can't possibly know what goes on in there. People use that forest for all sorts of things, hunting, camping, God knows what else. It isn't Lilly, I can tell you that much."

"No, ma'am, we didn't think so," Jackson injected smoothly. "Did your sister spend a lot of time out there? In the woods, I mean."

"She loved the woods and the animals. They were her friends, more so than most people." Mildred's voice grew wistful. "She had a way with creatures—could get a wild deer to eat from her hand, calm a frightened bird. Said the forest was the only place she felt truly free."

"Did she walk up and down the highway a lot?" Pressley set the cup of tea down, unable to stomach another sip of the bitter brew.

"T'weren't much else to do out this way back then. No television, no radio that worked proper. Our father told her it wasn't safe, that a young girl shouldn't be wandering around alone, especially after dark. He never forgave himself and started drinking heavily after she died. Blamed himself every day until the drink finally killed him." Mildred's rocking grew more agitated. "Like I said, our family wasn't the same after. All the joy left when my sister died, and it never came back."

The picture Mildred painted was heartbreaking. A tale of a family destroyed by one night of violence, never able to heal or move forward. But Pressley couldn't shake the feeling that there were still pieces missing from the story.

"Can you tell us about the night Ethan came looking for your sister?" Pressley tilted her head, studying the older woman's face for any telltale reactions. "It's very disturbing that we found all those bodies buried on your property. Surely you must have some idea how they got there."

Mildred frowned, her face flushing an angry red. "Do I look capable of digging a bunch of graves? That boy ran out of here like ghosts were chasing him, babbling about seeing Lilly and hearing voices. His brother wasn't much different when he came looking. Spooked as easily as a deer during hunting season." Her face grew redder, and she rocked faster, the chair creaking ominously. "I get what you're doing, trying to pin this on me. See yourself out. Since you aren't law enforcement, don't come back. I'll have my rifle handy if you do."

The threat was delivered with enough conviction to make Pressley believe the old woman meant every word. But as they prepared to leave, she noticed a loose thread on her pants that had caught what looked like a silver hair. Without thinking, she plucked it free.

Pressley stood, slipping the hair into her pocket with practiced discretion. "You know something about those bodies, ma'am, and we intend to find out what is going on here. Since it can't be Lilly flagging down young men the same time every year, it has to be someone else. I think you know exactly who that someone is."

"Think what you want. Won't change nothing."

"What a hateful woman," Pressley said once they returned to the car, her hands shaking slightly from the encounter.

"She knows something, and she's scared." Jackson started the car and backed away from the house, gravel crunching under the tires. "Let's pay Nate a visit. See what exactly spooked him when he was here."

"Wait a minute. Let's go back. I have more questions." Pressley put a hand on his arm.

"Do you want to get shot? She seemed serious about that rifle."

Pressley considered this, then shook her head. "There's something important we missed. Mildred never said how Lilly's body was found, or who found it. That might be crucial to understanding what happened that night."

"Okay, but be careful." He drove back to the house and stepped onto the porch with her, hand resting on his gun.

"Goodness, don't you two listen?" Mildred yanked the door open before they could knock, as if she'd been watching from the window.

"Almost finished. Who found your sister's body?"

"My father did. When she wasn't home by dark, he went looking for her. Searched all night before he found her in that ditch." She glanced over Pressley's shoulder and gave a slight shake of her head, so subtle it was almost imperceptible.

Pressley turned in time to see a figure in white melt into the shadows between the trees. The figure was too far away to make out details, but it moved with purpose rather than the random wandering of someone lost.

"Someone you know?"

"Who?" The woman's brow furrowed with what appeared to be genuine confusion. "I didn't see no one. Now git. Any more questions can come from the police." She slammed the door hard enough to rattle the windows.

"Did you see what I did, Jackson?" Pressley kept staring in the direction the figure had gone, hoping for another glimpse.

"Yep. Someone is playing a game I'm not sure we want to play. That little head shake she gave—she was signaling someone."

"We're going to have to play if we want answers. Let's go take a look." She headed in that direction only to have him pull her back.

"Nope. We don't know those woods, and whoever's in there does. We'd be at a disadvantage from the start."

Pressley sighed in frustration. If they didn't take more of an initiative, they'd never get to the bottom of Lilly's death or find Ethan's killer. "Maybe when we find out what's going on in there, we'll solve Lilly Hensley's murder. In order to do that, we're going to have to search those woods eventually."

"Not without being prepared. We stick out like a sore thumb in our street clothes."

She grinned, the first moment of levity she'd felt all day. "You want to wear black and use night vision goggles?"

"Sounds good to me. I want to solve this as much

as you do, but my main priority is keeping us alive to do so."

He again backed away from the house, then headed down the highway toward Nate's home. The drive gave them time to process what they'd learned. The Duvall house was a stark contrast to the Hensley place—well-maintained, modern, and filled with the warmth that came from a loving family. A red-eyed woman answered the door, and Jackson introduced himself and Pressley.

"We'd like to speak to Nate, please."

"Come in." She stepped back, her movements careful and controlled like someone holding herself together through sheer will. "He told us he hired some private investigators. Let me write you a check. At least we know what happened to our son, even if the knowing hurts more than the not knowing did."

"We intend to find his killer, ma'am." Pressley breathed deeply, trying to find the right words for a grieving mother.

"I've read about the two of you and how you solved that old murder case. The newspaper articles said you never give up until you find the truth." Her eyes brimmed with fresh tears. "I have faith that you will find justice for my Ethan. Please, have a seat." She motioned to a leather sofa that still held the indentations from family movie nights and homework sessions. "I'll get Nate."

The young man returned without his mother and a

check in his hand. His eyes were red-rimmed and haunted, aged years in the space of days. He gave the check to Pressley, then sat across from them, his movements careful as if sudden motions might shatter what remained of his composure. "You want to talk to me?"

"We've just left Miss Hensley's." Pressley folded the check and slid it into her pocket. They may have done what they were hired to do, but they weren't finished yet. Justice demanded more than just finding a body. "She said you seemed frightened when you were there. May we ask why?"

"Ghost stories freak me out." He looked away, his jaw clenching. "Always have, since I was a kid."

"You believe in ghosts?" She arched a brow.

"I didn't until I went there looking for Ethan." The color drained from his face, leaving him pale as parchment. "Now I don't know what to believe."

"What did you see?" Jackson leaned forward, his voice gentle but insistent.

"I felt like I was being watched from the moment I got out of my car. The old woman laughed and said not to worry because it wasn't prom night, like that was supposed to be comforting." He clenched his fists tight enough to turn his knuckles white. "I heard laughing coming from the woods—not normal laughter, but something that made my skin crawl. After I got in my car to leave, I looked back toward the trees. A dark-haired girl in a white dress smiled and waved at me, then beckoned me to follow her. I got out of there as fast as I could. No way was I going to follow a ghost into those woods. Look what happened to my brother."

"What you saw, Nate, was a flesh-and-blood girl," Pressley said firmly. "We've seen her too, and possibly others like her."

"She's after me now. I know it." He started to tremble, the shock of his brother's death finally breaking through his composure. "I see her in my dreams. I see my brother's face when they pulled him from that grave. Someone beat him to a pulp before they killed him."

More than one person in her opinion. Unless a woman used something heavy to bludgeon him with, she couldn't do that kind of damage alone. There wasn't an inch of the young man left without some kind of bruising—his face, his torso, even his hands showed signs of defensive wounds. Someone had tortured him before ending his life.

"We're going to find out who did this to him," Pressley promised.

He raised hopeful eyes. "But your job is done, isn't it? You found him."

"It isn't finished until we find out what happened to your brother and make sure whoever did this can't hurt anyone else." Jackson stood and placed a hand on Nate's shoulder. "You stay away from the Hensley place and surrounding woods, okay? Promise me."

"No need to tell me twice." He shuddered. "I heard

women whispering, laughing. They said Lilly's name over and over like some kind of chant. I felt them watching me as I sped away, following my car with their eyes."

"But you only saw one?" Pressley had seen more than one when the diggers had uncovered the bodies.

"Just the one, but I heard at least three different voices." His hands shook as he ran them through his hair. "What if they come after me? What if showing up there marked me somehow?"

Could it be a group of women killing the men—a club of some sort? Why? A twisted game of revenge that had been going on for decades? The idea seemed far-fetched, but everything about this case defied conventional logic.

Back in the car, she turned to Jackson. "We need to find out whether Mildred has relatives. I know she said she didn't, but nothing else makes sense." She grinned and patted her pocket. "I have a hair that I really hope belongs to her. DNA will tell us whether she has relatives, assuming any of them have been tested or arrested."

"You're brilliant." He pulled her close for a quick kiss. "Absolutely marvelous. I'm so glad we're partners."

"Yep. Because I'm sneakier than you are." Face flushed from both the compliment and the kiss, she straightened. Jackson, being a former law enforcement, made him more of a rule follower than she was, thankfully. Besides, the hair had been on her pants. She hadn't gone digging through Mildred's things. Technically.

Back at the office, she dropped the hair into a small Ziploc bag and packaged it carefully for shipping. Jackson had a contact at a private lab who could run DNA analysis off the books, no questions asked. They wouldn't find out anything for a few days, but at least they were moving forward. She sat in her office chair and propped her feet on her desk, finally allowing herself to feel the exhaustion of the past few days. "What now?"

Jackson glanced up from his computer, adjusting his reading glasses. "We have a few jobs lined up. If we want to keep the doors open, we'll have to earn some money in between finding Ethan's killer."

"What kind of jobs?" She hoped for something more interesting than their usual fare.

"One woman wants us to find out whether her husband is having an affair. Says he's been staying late at work and coming home smelling like perfume."

"I hate those kinds of cases." The work was necessary but soul-crushing, confirming people's worst fears about the ones they loved.

"Another is a business wanting to know whether an employee is faking a back injury. Man's been collecting worker's comp for six months, but the company thinks he's been doing construction work on weekends."

"A lot of times they are faking." Pressley twirled a

pencil through her fingers, a nervous habit she'd developed. She much preferred cold cases to these petty investigations, but Jackson was right. They had bills to pay and a reputation to maintain. She pulled the check from the Duvalls from her pocket and set it in her outgoing mail to take to the bank the next day.

What to do now? Pressley itched to go into the woods but knew better than to go alone. She'd have to wait until Jackson decided they were properly prepared. Too dangerous otherwise. The two of them couldn't take on multiple women at one time, especially ones with vengeance on their minds and decades of experience in these particular woods.

The bell over the door jingled, its cheerful sound incongruous with the dark thoughts filling Pressley's mind. She looked up from her desk, and her pencil dropped from nerveless fingers when she saw who had entered.

A young woman with dark hair and pale skin stood in the doorway, wearing a white dress that looked like it belonged in the 1940s. Her resemblance to the photos of Lilly Hensley was so striking it took Pressley's breath away. But this couldn't be Lilly—could it?

Chapter Five

Pressley bolted to her feet and pasted on a smile, though her heart was hammering against her ribs. "Welcome to Hudson and Taylor. May we help you?" She glanced at Jackson who looked as surprised as she did, his coffee mug frozen halfway to his lips.

The resemblance to the photographs of Lilly Hensley was uncanny—the same dark hair, the same delicate bone structure, even the same way of holding her head slightly tilted to one side. But this woman was alive, breathing, and standing in their office in modern times, despite wearing what looked like a vintage 1940s dress.

"I sure hope so." The woman kept her gaze on Jackson as most clients did when they entered the office. Pressley didn't blame them. She'd do the same with a man as handsome as her Jackson, though something about this woman's focused attention felt different—more calculating than appreciative. "My fiancé, Devin Finch, is missing."

"Do you have a photo?" Pressley managed to keep her voice steady, though her mind was racing with questions about the woman's identity and timing.

"Of course." She pulled a glossy 4 x 6 picture in a frame from her purse with practiced ease, as if she'd rehearsed this moment.

Wow. The man looked like one of those generic models that came with picture frames. Too perfect, too posed, with the kind of artificial smile that photographers coached their subjects to produce. "Please, have a seat and tell us all you can. Would you like a cup of coffee, water, or soda?"

"Water would be wonderful." She smiled as Jackson moved his chair closer, and Pressley noticed that the woman's eyes never left his face, studying his reactions with the intensity of someone conducting her own interview. "I've been told you're the best private investigators in this part of Arkansas."

Pressley frowned at being relegated to the role of refreshment server. Apparently, this was going to be Jackson's interview, at least from the client's perspective. She grabbed a clean mug from the break-room cabinet, filled it with water from the cooler, and returned to set it in front of the potential new client. The woman's fingers were long and elegant, but Pressley noticed calluses that suggested she worked with her hands regularly. She then printed off a contract and handed it to her to sign, noting how the woman's penmanship was deliberately neat, as if she were being extra careful with her writing.

"We do our best, ma'am." Jackson flashed his pearly whites again, though Pressley could see the wariness in his eyes. Years of police work had given him excellent instincts about people, and something was bothering him about this woman. "What is your name, and when was the last time you saw your fiancé?"

"I'm Amara Jones." She took a sip of the water, and Pressley noticed that no diamond ring winked from her finger. No tan line showed she'd ever worn one either, which was odd for someone claiming to be recently engaged. "Last Friday, the night I broke things off with him. I went to his apartment the next morning to collect my things, but he wasn't there. Every day since, I've gone to his place, tried calling…nothing." She removed an envelope from her purse and counted out five hundred dollars in cash for the retaining fee, the bills crisp and new as if they'd come straight from a bank.

Who kept that much money in their purse? Pressley had learned over the years that people who paid in large amounts of cash were often trying to avoid leaving a paper trail. The woman's story was already raising red flags, and they'd barely gotten started.

"His address?" Jackson motioned for Pressley to write it down as the woman recited the address to an apartment complex in town. He leaned back in his chair, his posture casual but his eyes alert. "This is a personal question, but why did you call off the engagement?"

Tears sprang to her dark eyes with surprising suddenness, though something about them seemed rehearsed. "I found out he'd been seeing someone else. Caught him with her. It broke my heart."

Who in their right mind would cheat on a woman as beautiful as Amara? The story felt too convenient, too perfectly tragic. While Jackson continued the interview, Pressley typed the address into her phone's GPS, noting that the apartment complex was only a couple of miles away. Convenient for someone who might need to create a believable cover story quickly.

"Do you think he might've been lured by the…ghost of that girl who died out there?" Amara blinked away the tears, and Pressley caught something in her expression—a flicker of satisfaction, perhaps, or anticipation.

The question sent chills down Pressley's spine. How would this woman know about the Lilly Hensley case unless she'd been following their investigation? The discovery of the bodies had made the local news, but the ghost angle hadn't been widely reported.

"Ghosts aren't real, ma'am." Jackson shook his head firmly. "Ghosts can't lure or kill. Can you tell us anything else about him? About his friends and family?"

"He didn't have any friends, and he was an only

child. Both his parents were dead." She took a deep breath, as if the admission caused her pain. "I'm not giving you much to go on, am I?"

"We've gone on less." Jackson stood and walked the woman to the door, his hand hovering near her elbow without quite touching her. Once she left, he turned to Pressley with a grim expression. "I thought for a second the ghost of Lilly Hensley had come to see us."

Pressley dumped the remaining water from the mug, then placed the mug carefully in a paper bag. "Let's send this in for DNA testing. If she's related to Mildred Hensley, we need to know."

"We can drop it off at the station on our way to check out this Devin character's apartment." Jackson grabbed his suit jacket from the back of his chair. "I'd bet my favorite pair of boots Amara Jones is related to the Hensleys. The resemblance is too strong to be coincidental."

The apartment manager, a thin man in his sixties with nervous hands, led them to Devin's supposed residence. The place didn't look lived in—more like a staged apartment for prospective renters, with generic furniture and no personal touches anywhere. The air smelled stale, as if windows hadn't been opened in months.

"You sure this is his place?" Pressley headed for the bedroom closet, her footsteps echoing in the empty-feeling space.

"Yes, ma'am. He isn't here much from what I gather. Travels for his work, he told me when he signed the lease. I've not ever seen him around the complex, though."

"Then how do you know he lives here?" She glanced over her shoulder, then opened the closet. Shirts, pants, and suits hung from the bar in perfect order. Each article of clothing was placed exactly the same space apart, as if arranged by someone with obsessive-compulsive tendencies—or someone trying to create the appearance of occupancy without actually living there.

"The former manager told me about him when I took over six months ago. Said he'd been a model tenant, always paid his rent on time, never caused any trouble."

"Hey, I've found some diner receipts in the desk drawer." Jackson pulled on a pair of rubber gloves, then held up the receipts. "Looks like he ate at the same diner regularly, if these are to be believed. All from Sunshine Diner on Main Street."

Pressley moved to the bathroom, noting that everything was positioned with the same unnatural precision as the closet. Nothing on the counter except a small hand towel folded into a perfect rectangle. The medicine cabinet held a toothbrush still in its packaging, travel-sized toothpaste that hadn't been opened, shaving cream with the price sticker still attached, and a disposable razor still wrapped in plastic.

No medications, no prescription bottles, nothing that suggested someone used this bathroom. On a shelf in the walk-in shower sat a new bar of soap, still in its wrapper. Maybe they'd get more information from the nearby diner, because this apartment was telling them nothing except that someone had gone to great lengths to create the illusion of occupancy.

They thanked the apartment manager and drove to Sunshine Diner, which looked like an old railroad car converted into a restaurant. The chrome exterior gleamed in the afternoon sun, and the smell of fried food drifted from the kitchen. After the waitress led them to a red vinyl booth that had seen better days, Pressley showed her the photo of Devin.

"I don't think I've ever seen him before." The waitress, a woman in her forties with tired eyes and comfortable shoes, studied the photo carefully. "Hey, Ashley, can you come look at this?"

Another waitress joined them, this one younger with bleached blonde hair pulled back in a ponytail. "He looks a little familiar, maybe. But I see a lot of faces every day."

"You don't recognize someone who supposedly comes in here every day during the supper hour?" Pressley held the photo closer, watching the women's faces for any sign of recognition. "Look again, please. This is important."

"Well, he might be the man who comes in wearing a dark suit," Ashley said slowly, squinting at the photo.

"But that guy always sits in the corner booth and keeps to himself. Never really got a good look at his face, and he always pays cash and leaves before I can clear his table."

Pressley sighed and returned the photo to her bag. The description was so vague it could apply to dozens of men. "We'll question the surrounding stores. I'll take the lunch special—a BLT, please."

"Mushroom burger for me." Jackson leaned against the back of the booth, his expression troubled. "I don't think this is going to be easy. Everything about this case feels manufactured."

"It's almost as if the man doesn't exist." Pressley had learned to trust her gut over the years, and right now it was telling her they were being led on a wild goose chase. The question was why. Who would go to such elaborate lengths to create a fake missing person case, and what did they hope to accomplish? Still, they needed to follow every lead, no matter how suspicious it seemed.

They spent the next two hours canvassing the surrounding stores, a pharmacy, a hardware store, a small grocery market, and a dry cleaner. Nobody recognized Devin's photo, despite the apartment manager's claim that he was often seen in the neighborhood. Jackson called a former colleague at the police department and asked him to run a search on Devin Finch. "He'll get back to us when he's found something, if there's anything to find."

"Now what?" Pressley asked as they returned to their car.

"Let's head back to the office and see whether we can find anything on social media about Amara or Devin. Sometimes people reveal more about themselves online than they realize."

Back at the office, Pressley settled at her computer and typed in Amara's name. Her online presence looked suspiciously new—she only had a handful of followers, all of whom seemed to be fake accounts with generic profile pictures and no post history. Her photos were mostly selfies taken in nondescript locations, and there was no mention of a fiancé, family, or even friends. Pressley couldn't find anything that couldn't have been slapped together online in a couple of hours by someone with basic computer skills. "Any luck finding Devin?"

"Nope." Jackson rolled his head on his shoulders, trying to work out the tension that had been building all day. "The man has absolutely no online presence. No Facebook, no Instagram, no LinkedIn, no Twitter. In this day and age, that's almost impossible unless someone is deliberately trying to stay invisible."

"Amara has very little presence either, and what she does have looks fake."

"She didn't seem very worried about her missing fiancé to me," he said thoughtfully. "The tears looked forced, and her body language was all wrong for someone genuinely concerned about a loved one."

"I got the same impression. And why did she come to us instead of the police? She didn't say anything about going to the local authorities first, which is what most people would do."

"That's easy enough to verify." Jackson made the call, speaking in low tones with someone at the station. He hung up a minute later with a frown. "She didn't go to the police. They've never seen or heard from her before today." The phone on his desk rang, and he answered it quickly. "Hudson and Taylor Investigations. Really? That is strange. Thanks for your help, buddy." Jackson hung up and turned to Pressley with a grim expression. "Devin Finch doesn't seem to exist anywhere in the system. No social security number, no driver's license, no birth certificate, no employment records. Nothing."

"I thought his photo looked like it came with the frame." She drummed her fingers on the desk, a nervous habit that helped her think. "Let's call it a day. Maybe something will come to mind by morning. We know Amara exists. We've met her and have her DNA on that mug. All we have to do is find her and ask her why she lied to us."

The next morning, Pressley jotted down the address Amara had given on her contract, squinting at the woman's handwriting. She frowned as she tried to decipher the words. Pressley had lived in the area for several years and didn't recognize the street name. Another dead end? Probably, given their luck with this case so far. "We're supposed to go to Culver Street, but I've never heard of it."

"Neither have I." Jackson set a cup of coffee on her desk, the steam rising in lazy spirals. "And I grew up around here."

"My GPS has never heard of it either." She glared at her phone as if it were personally responsible for the confusion. "Her handwriting is atrocious. Maybe I read it wrong?"

Jackson pulled up a map of the area on his computer, adjusting his reading glasses. "Might be Chapel or Dover—both are long stretches from the word Culver, but they're the best I can come up with given the chicken scratch she calls handwriting. Let me see the contract."

She handed it to him, watching as he studied the scrawled address. "What do you think it says?"

"Looks like it could be Clover, maybe." His brow furrowed in concentration. "Let's try searching for just the house number and see what comes up." He typed the number into his search engine and waited for results. "Interesting. Five houses in town have that number."

"Let's go, then. We might have just found Ethan's killer." She grabbed her bag and jacket, adrenaline starting to pump through her system.

"At least we know Amara exists in some form. My buddy at the precinct found her driver's license in the system." Jackson held the door open for her. "But here's the interesting part—the address he gave me from her license isn't one of the five we found, and he said the house at that address has been vacant for years. Condemned, actually."

"I can't believe I'm saying this, but if we do find her, we need to let the police know immediately. She could be the primary suspect in this case." She climbed into the car, buckling her seatbelt. "Why else would she go to all these elaborate lengths to lie to us?"

"Want to stop by the station first? Let Detective Anderson know what we're doing?"

"He'll probably tell us to stop investigating and leave it to the professionals."

Jackson shook his head as he started the engine. "He'll probably be glad to let us do the footwork. His department is understaffed and overworked."

Detective Anderson glared at them from across his cluttered desk when they explained their morning's discovery. Empty coffee cups and case files covered every available surface, and the fluorescent lighting made everyone look slightly green. "I thought I told you two to let us handle the investigation from here on out."

"This woman came to us, Detective." A muscle ticked in Jackson's jaw, and Pressley could see him struggling to maintain his professional demeanor. "Not one bit of her story has checked out. The missing man doesn't exist, the address she gave us is fake, and she paid us five hundred dollars in cash for what appears to be a completely fabricated case. Do you want our help or not?"

Anderson waved a hand in dismissal, as if brushing away an annoying fly. "Go ahead and chase down your leads. This office has a full caseload already, and we don't have the manpower to hunt down addresses that most likely don't exist anyway." He narrowed his eyes and pointed a finger at them. "But if you find her, do not—and I cannot stress this enough—do not approach her directly. Call us immediately. We don't want her spooked and taking off before we can question her properly."

"Got it." Jackson put a hand on the small of Pressley's back and guided her back outside, both of them breathing easier once they were away from Anderson's hostile energy.

"He's an unpleasant man," Pressley said, cutting a glance over her shoulder toward the station. "You'd think the police would appreciate the help of experienced investigators. The more people working a case, the faster it gets solved."

"As a former police officer, I can attest to the fact that some private investigators are ill-trained and only complicate things," Jackson said with a rueful smile. "They contaminate crime scenes, interfere with witnesses, and generally make a mess of everything they touch." He smiled at her over the top of the car. "You're a notable exception to that rule, sweetheart."

She grinned back at him. "Gee, thanks. I think that

was a compliment buried in there somewhere."

They spent the next several hours driving to each of the five addresses, finding nothing but confused homeowners who had never heard of Amara Jones or Devin Finch. But as luck would have it, as they were heading back to the office, they spotted her coming out of the grocery store with a cart full of food, enough groceries to feed several people for a month.

Jackson parked a few cars down and immediately phoned Detective Anderson. "We found her," he said quietly. "Bill's Market on Fifth Street. She's loading groceries into a blue Honda Civic."

Before Amara had finished loading her groceries into her trunk, a squad car pulled up with lights flashing. Two officers got out, spoke briefly with her, then ushered her into the backseat. The patrol car headed toward the police department, and Amara's car was left in the parking lot.

"We are going to follow, right?" Pressley craned her neck in the direction the police car had gone. "I'm sure Anderson will let us watch the interrogation."

"You bet we're going to follow." Jackson whipped the car around and sped toward the station, his jaw set with determination.

The detective frowned when they asked to observe the questioning, but he finally nodded grudgingly. "Stay behind the two-way mirror. Do not, under any circumstances, come into the interrogation room. Neither of you belongs in there, and I don't want any complications that could compromise this case in court." He straightened his tie and shoved open the door to the interrogation room.

The room was stark and windowless, with fluorescent lighting that cast harsh shadows. Anderson sat across from Amara, who looked remarkably composed for someone who had just been brought in for questioning.

"Miss Jones, we're aware of the fact that you hired Hudson and Taylor Investigations to find a Devin Finch." Anderson folded his hands on the metal table between them. "A man who, according to our research, does not exist. Mind telling us why you would create such an elaborate fiction?"

"Not without a lawyer." She hitched her chin defiantly, and Pressley noticed that her earlier nervousness had completely disappeared.

"Do you have a lawyer?"

"No, but I know my rights."

"We can get a public defender for you if you'd like. Would you prefer that?"

"I want my phone call first." She glanced directly at the two-way mirror, as if she knew precisely where Pressley and Jackson were standing.

"You aren't under arrest, ma'am." The unspoken "yet" hung heavy in the air between them.

"Then why am I here?" She crossed her arms and leaned back in the metal chair. "If I'm not under arrest, you can't legally detain me or continue questioning me against my will."

"So sue me," Anderson said bluntly. "Here are the facts as I see them: One, you look uncannily like the late Lilly Hensley, whose case we're actively investigating. Two, multiple bodies were found buried on Hensley property, all young men. Three, you hired private investigators to locate someone who doesn't exist, paying them five hundred dollars in cash. All of this looks very suspicious from where I'm sitting. Do you know Mildred Hensley?"

Pressley shot a surprised look at Jackson. "I wasn't aware he suspected Mildred the way we do."

"It's a good thing he's thinking along the same lines," Jackson replied quietly. "Means we won't be working at cross-purposes."

"No, I don't know any Mildred Hensley." Amara's gaze shifted to the left as she spoke—a classic tell that she was lying.

Anderson exhaled heavily, his patience clearly wearing thin. "I'm going to ask you one more time, and I suggest you think carefully before you answer. Why did you hire Hudson and Taylor on what appears to be a completely fabricated case?"

A sly smile stretched across Amara's lips, transforming her face from innocent to something far more calculating. "I had nothing better to do and five hundred dollars burning a hole in my purse. Is curiosity a crime now?"

Anderson's face darkened, and his hands clenched

into fists on the table. He looked as if he wanted to reach across and throttle the woman. "Stop playing games, Miss Jones, before I find a reason to lock you up."

"On what charge?" She kept her smile in place and tilted her head mockingly. "No harm was done, and the investigators are five hundred dollars richer for their trouble. Seems like everyone won. Can I go now?"

Anderson stared at her in tense silence for a long moment, his jaw working as if he were chewing on words he couldn't say. Finally, he nodded curtly. "Don't leave town, Miss Jones. Put your real address on this piece of paper, and it had better be the truth this time."

She scrawled down an address with deliberate slowness, then pushed to her feet with fluid grace. "Tell the investigators I wish them luck in their investigation. They're going to need it."

"Tell them yourself."

Amara's eyes widened with what looked like genuine surprise as she stepped from the interrogation room to find Pressley and Jackson standing in the hallway. "Well, well. Enjoy the show?" She arched a perfectly sculpted brow.

"Very much," Pressley replied with a grin that didn't reach her eyes. "We'll be seeing you again, Amara. You can count on it." The woman was involved in what happened to Ethan, and Pressley wouldn't stop until she found out exactly how deep Amara's involvement went.

Chapter Six

Pressley's hands trembled as she slipped on the night vision goggles and followed Jackson into the dark woods near the Hensley house. The cool plastic pressed against her face, and she adjusted the strap with nervous fingers. She hefted the small backpack she wore more securely on her shoulders, feeling the weight of the water bottles, first aid kit, and evidence bags they'd packed for this expedition. The only light other than the sliver of moon was the green glow of Jackson's cell phone as he followed a topographical map of the area he'd downloaded earlier.

They'd spent the afternoon preparing for this nighttime reconnaissance, studying satellite images and planning their route. Jackson had insisted they go in prepared—extra batteries for their equipment, backup flashlights, and even flares in case they got separated. His police training showed in every detail of their preparation, from the way he'd mapped out multiple exit routes to his insistence that they check in with Detective Anderson before heading out.

The forest felt different at night, more alive and somehow malevolent. The only sounds were the occasional rustle of leaves underfoot and the distant call of an owl, its haunting cry echoing through the trees. Every shadow seemed to harbor potential threats, and Pressley found herself jumping at the slightest noise. Near where they'd seen the women in white before, they stopped. Jackson set up a motion-sensor camera with practiced efficiency, camouflaging it among the branches of a large oak tree, then led Pressley into a thick stand of bushes that provided good cover while offering a clear view of the path.

An hour passed without incident, the minutes crawling by with agonizing slowness. Pressley's legs cramped from crouching in the same position, and she began to wonder if they were wasting their time as they had the last couple of days. They'd made three previous attempts to catch sight of the mysterious women, but each time had come up empty-handed. Maybe the figures only appeared when they weren't actively looking for them.

Jackson stiffened suddenly, his entire body going rigid with alertness. "Do you see that?" He whispered and pointed down the path with a gloved hand.

At first, she couldn't make out what he'd seen through the green haze of the night vision goggles, but then a figure emerged from the darkness—pale and draped in what appeared to be a flowing white dress that seemed to move independently of any breeze. The figure stood perfectly still for a long moment, her face obscured by long, dark hair that hung like a curtain around her shoulders.

Pressley shuddered, her breath catching in her throat. Even through the technological enhancement of the goggles, there was something deeply unsettling about the woman's stillness. "Do we wait to see if others join her?"

"Yes," Jackson breathed, his voice barely audible.

The woman drifted across the path with an otherworldly grace, seeming to glide rather than walk. Her feet made no sound on the forest floor, and her movements had an ethereal quality that made Pressley's skin crawl. She gripped Jackson's arm tightly. "We have to follow her," she whispered, knowing it was probably a mistake but unable to resist the compulsion.

They stepped carefully onto the path, their boots crunching softly on fallen leaves despite their attempts at stealth. The woman had disappeared as silently as she'd appeared, leaving no trace of her passage except for a faint scent in the air. Something floral and cloying that reminded Pressley of funeral flowers. Her nerves were on edge, every sense heightened by adrenaline and fear. They weren't the only ones out here, and she had the distinct feeling unseen eyes were watching them.

The sounds of the night seemed amplified through their heightened awareness—the snap of a branch somewhere in the distance, the skitter of a small animal fleeing through the underbrush, the rustle of leaves that might have been wind or might have been something else entirely. Her heart pounded so loudly she was sure it would give away their position, and she kept a hand firmly pressed against Jackson's back, drawing comfort from his solid presence.

They stopped when Jackson spotted a set of tire tracks pressed deep into the soft earth. He knelt and ran his hand along the ground with the careful attention of someone trained in evidence collection. "These are fresh. Maybe a day or two old at most."

"Look." Pressley motioned to a piece of fabric fluttering from a tree branch about six feet off the ground. Its stark whiteness contrasted sharply with the inkiness of the night, standing out like a beacon in their night vision. She reached up and plucked it free, noting the fine quality of the material—silk, possibly, or some other expensive fabric. She placed it carefully in her backpack, making sure not to contaminate it with her bare hands.

The tracks beckoned them deeper into the woods, leading away from any established trail and into the heart of the forest. Whispers, so faint she thought she might be imagining them, seemed to swirl around them on the night air, urging them to turn back even as curiosity and professional duty drove them forward. The voices were indistinct, but something was menacing about their tone that made the hair on the back of Pressley's neck stand up.

A loud crack echoed behind them, sharp and sudden in the relative quiet. Jackson immediately pulled a hunting knife from his pocket and stepped protectively in front of Pressley, his body tense and ready for confrontation.

"I don't like this." Pressley grabbed his arm, her voice tight with anxiety. "This feels like a trap."

"Probably just a deer," he said, but his grip on the knife remained firm.

She wasn't so sure. The crack had sounded too deliberate, too perfectly timed to their passage. When nothing appeared after several tense minutes, they turned to continue following the tracks. Pressley couldn't shake the sensation of being watched, as if hostile eyes were tracking their every movement through the darkness.

The deeper they went, the stranger the forest became. They'd long since left the familiar territory around the Hensley house behind, venturing into areas that felt wild and untouched by human presence. The trees grew thicker here, their branches intertwining overhead to block out even the faint moonlight. Pressley stopped abruptly at the sight of scorch marks in the soil, dark patches where something had burned hot enough to sterilize the earth. Pieces of broken glass glinted among the ashes, catching the green light of their goggles like malevolent eyes. "Something happened here." Her voice carried a mix of fear and fascination.

Jackson bent down to examine the area more closely, his flashlight beam revealing details their goggles had missed. "Though I get the feeling we're not supposed to find out what." He lifted a remnant of frayed rope that had been tied around a nearby tree, the fibers dark with what might have been blood. "This might be where the men were taken and killed."

"Like some kind of ritual sacrifice?"

"Maybe. The positioning of these burn marks isn't random—look how they form a rough circle."

Pressley studied the pattern, noting the deliberate spacing of the scorched areas. "Do you think we're being purposefully led here? I mean, if we're dealing with a group of women who hate men…and you're a man—"

"The thought has crossed my mind more than once," Jackson admitted, straightening to scan the surrounding trees. "But I'm not those young men who were killed. I'm trained, armed, and alert. They won't catch me unaware like they did the others."

"You'd still be outnumbered if there are as many of them as we suspect."

After a short walk that felt like miles, they came upon a clearing that took Pressley's breath away. The grass had been flattened and even worn down to the dirt in spots, as if many feet had passed this way repeatedly over a long period. In the center lay a large, jagged circle of charred earth that had to be at least ten feet in diameter. Surrounding it were strange symbols etched into the dirt, some barely legible after exposure to the elements, but unmistakably deliberate and purposeful.

Pressley crouched down, running her fingers over one of the carvings. The symbol looked vaguely familiar, like something she might have seen in a book about folklore or ancient religions. "Definitely ritualistic. These aren't random scratches—someone spent time creating these."

She stood and studied the remnants of what must have been a massive fire pit. A burned piece of paper stuck up from the ashes like a tiny gravestone. She bent down to read it, but the words were too damaged by fire and weather to be deciphered. Only fragments of letters remained, tantalizing hints of whatever message had once been written there. "This isn't a random spot." Her eyes lifted and scanned the dark perimeter of the clearing. She whispered, her voice shaking with the weight of realization. "We were led here deliberately. Someone is giving us a message, showing us something they want us to see."

A loud snap made them both freeze, the sound unnaturally sharp in the oppressive silence of the clearing. Jackson removed his night vision goggles and turned on his high-powered flashlight, its beam cutting through the darkness like a sword. The sudden white light was blinding after the green glow of the goggles, and Pressley blinked rapidly as her eyes adjusted. But despite the powerful beam, she couldn't see anything beyond the immediate circle of illumination. The silence that followed the crack was deafening, pregnant with unseen menace.

"I think we should head back, Jackson." The words came out more urgently than she'd intended.

"Just a little further. I saw something through the trees—looked like it might be a structure of some kind."

Pressley's mind screamed at her not to go further, every instinct warning her that they were walking into danger. But she didn't want to be left alone in this cursed place, so she reluctantly followed him deeper into the woods. She kept glancing over her shoulder as they went, certain that something was following them just outside the range of their light.

They came across an abandoned vintage vehicle that looked like it had been sitting in the forest for decades. Rust had eaten through the metal body in several places, creating holes that looked like diseased wounds. The tires had long ago deflated and rotted away, leaving the car sitting on its rims. Vines snaked through the broken windows like grasping fingers, and the trunk hung open as if the car had been frozen in the act of screaming.

Jackson shined his flashlight inside the vehicle's interior. The seats had been torn apart and covered in mold, their stuffing scattered across the floor like the entrails of some mechanical beast. A piece of fabric, identical to the one she carried in her backpack, taunted her from a shard of glass left in the passenger window. The material fluttered in a breeze she couldn't feel, and she pulled it free with trembling fingers, adding it to her growing collection of evidence.

A low, mournful sound rose from somewhere deeper in the woods—a long, drawn-out moan that seemed to reverberate through the trees and penetrate to the very core of her being. The sound was neither quite human nor altogether animal, but something in between that made her blood run cold. "I've never heard an animal make a sound like that." Pressley gripped Jackson's hand so tightly she was probably cutting off his circulation.

"Me neither. Let's get out of here. Now."

Finally. They retraced their steps as quickly as they dared, racing through the forest as fast as the terrain and darkness would allow. Jackson stopped long enough to grab the motion-sensor camera on their way past, not wanting to leave any evidence of their presence behind. By the time they reached Jackson's car, their breath came in ragged gasps and their clothes were soaked with perspiration despite the cool night air. Pressley yanked the passenger door open with such force she nearly tore it off its hinges. She couldn't get inside fast enough, slamming the door and immediately locking it as if that flimsy barrier could protect them from whatever lurked in those woods.

As they drove away, gravel spraying behind them in their haste to escape, she glanced in the side mirror and gasped. A woman in white, looking disturbingly similar to Amara, stood right at the edge of the tree line. As Pressley watched, the figure stepped backward and disappeared from sight, melting into the shadows as if she'd never been there at all.

"What's wrong?" Jackson asked, noticing her sharp intake of breath.

"I'm pretty sure I saw Amara as we drove away. She was standing there watching us leave." Pressley's hands shook as she gripped the door handle. "What kind of message do you think they're trying to send us?"

His jaw tightened as he accelerated down the dark highway. "We're being warned away. The question is whether we heed the warning or dig deeper."

Back at Pressley's apartment, she spread out the pieces of fabric and burned paper on her kitchen table under the bright overhead light. Everything looked more mundane in the familiar surroundings, but she could still feel the lingering dread from their expedition. Jackson put the camera's memory card into her laptop, and they waited anxiously for the images to load.

"They're loaded." He turned the laptop so she could see the screen, and they both leaned in to examine the results.

The photo of the figure in white was blurry but unmistakable, confirming that what they'd seen was human rather than some trick of light and shadow. The image sent a shiver down Pressley's spine despite the warmth of her apartment. "Does it look like she's wearing a wedding dress to you?" She picked up one of the pieces of fabric they'd found, holding it up to the light. "The material feels expensive—silk or maybe satin."

Jackson sat back in his chair, rubbing his temples. "So, we have a group of brides who hate men and kill any they can get their hands on? It sounds like something out of a B-grade horror movie."

"I'm not discounting anything at this point." She set the scrap of fabric back down on the table, treating it like the evidence it might prove to be. "I wonder if Lilly was supposed to be getting married around the time she was killed. What if she was murdered right before her wedding, and that's what started all this?"

He frowned, considering the possibility. "I doubt she'd have been walking down the highway in her wedding gown, though. That doesn't make sense."

Pressley pursed her lips, acknowledging the logic of his argument. "You're right about that." She sat down at her laptop and typed Lilly's name into the search engine, this time focusing on newspaper articles dated in the weeks and months before her death. Back in the 1940s, a wedding announcement would have been big news in a small town, especially for a family as prominent as the Hensleys appeared to have been.

Jackson used a magnifying glass to study the fragment of burned paper they'd recovered, squinting at the damaged text. "I think I can make out part of a word on this note—looks like 'Sa' followed by some letters I can't decipher."

"What do you think it means? Salvation…sacrifice…someone's name?"

He shrugged, setting down the magnifying glass with a frustrated sigh. "Just another piece that doesn't seem to fit the puzzle yet."

"Wait—bingo!" Pressley pointed at her computer screen. "Lilly was supposed to marry a Benjamin Perry two days after the date she was killed. Look at this engagement announcement from three weeks before her death."

"What happened to this Benjamin character after she died?"

She scrolled through later articles, searching for any mention of the grieving fiancé. "Here it is—says he was devastated over his loss and left town right after the funeral. Never came back, according to this follow-up article from a year later."

"He wouldn't still be alive by now, even if we could track him down." Jackson pushed to his feet, wincing slightly as the movement aggravated his headache. "I'm going to bunk on your sofa tonight if it's okay with you. I want to go back to those woods in the daylight tomorrow. See what we missed in the dark."

"Okay," she agreed, though going back there was the last thing she wanted to do. But Jackson was right. They needed to conduct a thorough search of the area, and daylight would reveal details they'd missed in their nighttime exploration.

The next morning dawned clear and bright, making their midnight adventure seem almost like a bad dream. They drove back to the forest and followed the same tire tracks they'd discovered the night before. Things didn't seem nearly as scary in the daylight, though Pressley couldn't shake the memory of that mournful cry echoing through the trees. They returned to the clearing to conduct a more thorough search, photographing everything and collecting additional cvidence.

Pressley stopped when she saw something glinting near the edge of the charred circle. A small, silver locket lay half buried in the dirt, its chain tangled around a root. A locket she recognized from the engagement photo of Lilly Hensley that had appeared in the newspaper. She carefully pried it open with her fingernail to reveal a small photograph of a young man with kind eyes and a gentle smile. Benjamin Perry, she'd wager her last dollar on it. "Why would Lilly's locket be out here, decades after her death?"

"No idea, but it's significant." Jackson photographed the locket in situ before she picked it up. "We need to get all the things we've collected to Detective Anderson. This is way beyond what we can handle on our own."

As they prepared to leave the clearing, Pressley noticed deep scratches on the bark of a nearby tree. The marks looked fresh, as if they'd been made recently with something sharp—claws or perhaps a knife. She snapped a photo before running her fingers over the gouges, feeling how deep they went into the wood. "These are new, Jackson. Made within the last day or two."

A flicker of white flashed through the trees at the edge of her vision. Before either of them could react, Jackson suddenly grabbed the back of his head and stumbled forward, then fell to his knees with a grunt of pain. He rolled over, pulling his weapon from its holster with practiced speed despite his disorientation. "Something hit me—felt like a rock. Can you see whoever threw it?"

"No." Pressley peered through the brush, scanning for any sign of movement. "Whoever it was is gone already. Are you hurt badly?"

He put a hand to the back of his head and winced when his fingers came away bloody. "Just a bump, I think, but it's a good one."

"Do we give chase?"

"No point. Whoever threw the rock is long gone by now." He got carefully to his feet, swaying slightly. "It's another warning, but these warnings only make me want to dig deeper. Tomorrow, we start questioning the old-timers left from Lilly's time. Someone in this town knows more than they're letting on."

They drove directly to the police station and turned over everything they'd found—the fabric pieces, the burned paper, the photographs, and most importantly,

Lilly's locket. Detective Anderson listened without expression while they recounted the events of the previous evening and that morning, occasionally asking for clarification but mostly just taking notes. When they'd finished, he nodded grimly. "I'll send some officers out there to secure the scene and conduct a proper forensic examination. You sure you're okay, Hudson? That head wound looks like it might need stitches."

"Pun intended?" Jackson grinned despite his obvious discomfort.

"Maybe." The detective's lips twitched in what might have been amusement. "I do appreciate your help, although I have to admit I have no idea how to proceed with what you've brought me. Guess I'll have the officers ask around about female-revenge cults or whatever the hell this is supposed to be."

"It would explain all those graves we found," Jackson said, putting his hand to his head again. "Maybe I should go to the clinic after all. This headache is getting worse."

"I'll drive." Pressley held out her hand for the keys. "You might have a concussion, and the last thing we need is for you to wreck the car."

He frowned but dropped the keys into her palm without argument.

Sure enough, the emergency room doctor confirmed that Jackson had a mild concussion and ordered him to take it easy for at least forty-eight hours.

No strenuous activity, no driving, and someone needed to monitor him for signs of worsening symptoms.

"Taking it easy is not something I'm good at," he told Pressley as they left the clinic, a white bandage covering the stitches on the back of his head. "Not until we find out what's really going on and who killed Ethan and all those other young men."

"Well, you're going to have to learn," Pressley replied firmly. "I need you healthy if we're going to solve this case."

Hopefully, they could do so without further injury to either of them, though given what they'd discovered so far, she wasn't optimistic about their chances.

Chapter Seven

Pressley jolted awake to the sound of shattering glass and the piercing wail of her alarm system cutting through the pre-dawn darkness. The shrill electronic screech sent adrenaline flooding through her system, and she threw off her covers without thinking. Not taking the time to put on slippers or a robe over her pajamas, she raced downstairs to the office, her bare feet slapping against the cold wooden steps.

The scene that greeted her was worse than she'd imagined. Her backpack had been dumped unceremoniously on the table, its contents scattered across the surface like the remnants of a ransacked life. Shards of glass from the front window littered the floor, catching the streetlight from outside and creating a dangerous carpet of sharp edges. The cool night air flowed through the broken window, carrying with it the scent of rain and something else. Something that reminded her of the funeral flowers she'd smelled in the woods.

She grabbed her desk phone with trembling fingers and called Jackson after she punched the code to shut off the alarm; the sudden silence was almost as jarring as the noise had been. "Someone broke into the office," she said without preamble when he answered on the first ring.

"Are you okay?" His voice was alert despite the early hour, and she could hear him moving around, probably already getting dressed.

"Yes, I'm fine. Shaken but unhurt."

"Good. I'll be there as soon as I can, but I've got problems of my own. Someone slashed all four of my tires and gouged deep scratches down the side of my truck with something sharp—looks like it might have been a knife or maybe claws." His voice carried a grim anger that she'd rarely heard from him. "They left a note under my windshield wiper that said to stay away from what's buried, written in what looks like red ink. Or maybe blood. I need to call the police about the vandalism. You should call them too."

"I will. Please be careful, Jackson." She returned to the safety of her apartment before placing the call, double-checking the locks on her door and windows. An officer would be here soon, but until then, she felt exposed and vulnerable.

Thank goodness she and Jackson had turned over most of their evidence to Detective Anderson the day before. She had no doubt in her mind that's what the intruder had been looking for—the fabric pieces, the photographs, anything that might lead back to the White Veil Society or whoever was behind these murders.

Her gaze fell on the leather-bound Bible on her coffee table, a gift from her grandmother that she hadn't opened in months. It had been a while since she'd turned to faith for guidance, but with the evil that seemed to be hovering over this case like a dark cloud, now might be the time to seek divine help. She opened the Bible at random, her finger landing on a passage in Psalms about protection from enemies and read until the police announced their presence downstairs with a firm knock. Feeling more at peace after saying a prayer for guidance and protection for both herself and Jackson, she went down to meet them.

"Detective Anderson wanted me to let you know the department has dug up some history on rumors of a women's vigilante group dating way back to the 1960s," one of the officers said after he'd finished taking pictures of the damage and dusting for fingerprints. He was a young man with earnest eyes who looked like he'd rather be anywhere else at four in the morning. "If you have time today, you might want to visit the library. The woman who works there, Mrs. Patterson, is an avid local historian. She might have information that could help your investigation."

Pressley tilted her head, feeling a familiar flash of

irritation. "He wants us to do more of his footwork instead of having his people follow up on leads?"

The officer shrugged apologetically. "We're stretched pretty thin with budget cuts and three officers out on medical leave. There's no one to spare chasing down rumors that might or might not pan out, especially when the crimes seem to happen only once a year. Besides, it'll be a whole year before prom rolls around again and someone else disappears."

If Pressley oversaw law enforcement in this county, she'd shut down Highway 365 every prom night and post guards at both ends. "Thanks for the suggestion. We'll look into it."

"Here's a business card for an honest window repair company—they do good work at fair prices. Have a good day, ma'am, and be careful. Whoever did this might come back."

"You too, officer." She watched him leave, then glanced out through the broken window to see Jackson pulling up in the sedan they used for business rather than his damaged truck. Once he entered the office, stepping carefully around the glass, she told him the news the officer had passed on from Anderson. "Looks like we know what we're doing today. I'll run upstairs and get dressed properly."

"We can grab breakfast on the way to the library." He frowned at the glass scattered across the floor, his expression dark with anger. "Bring down a broom and dustpan, and I'll clean up this mess while you get ready."

She brought him the cleaning supplies, then returned upstairs to dress in jeans and a sweater, choosing practical boots in case they ended up traipsing through the woods again. What did she and Jackson know that warranted someone breaking into their office and damaging Jackson's truck? It had to mean they were getting close to finding out something important, something that threatened whoever was behind these murders. Rumors always had a grain of truth attached to them, so there must be some organized group of women out there killing men. Women who all resembled Lilly Hensley in some way.

Why had the warning been left with Jackson and not here at the office? Was he being specifically singled out because he was a man? Would he be the next victim, despite it not being close to next year's prom? The thought sent cold fear racing through her veins.

She shared her suspicions with Jackson when they waited in the drive-thru line of a fast-food restaurant after ordering breakfast burritos and coffee. The normalcy of the morning routine felt surreal after the night's events. "Maybe we should step back and let Anderson handle all this himself from here on out. We did find Ethan, which was what we were originally paid to do."

A frown puckered his forehead, deepening the lines around his eyes. "No, I think we should see this through to the end. We're too close to solving this to quit now."

"But you were injured yesterday, and now they're escalating their threats—"

"We aren't quitting, Pressley." He sent her a sharp look that brooked no argument. "This isn't just about Ethan anymore. There are dozens of victims and potentially more to come."

"Fine." She crossed her arms and stared out the passenger window at the ordinary suburban landscape, so different from the dark woods where evil lurked. Stubborn man. She wasn't normally a quitter, her investigative instincts usually drove her to pursue a story to its conclusion, but the thought of something serious happening to Jackson sent ice through her veins.

When they arrived at the Redwood Public Library, a modest brick building that had served the community for over fifty years, the librarian's eyes grew wide behind her wire-rimmed glasses when Pressley explained what they were looking for. Mrs. Patterson was a woman in her sixties with silver hair pulled back in a neat bun and the kind of sharp intelligence that came from decades of research and fact-checking.

"Oh my, yes. I know exactly what group you're talking about. They call themselves The White Veil Society." She typed rapidly on her computer keyboard, her fingers flying over the keys with practiced efficiency. "You really think they're behind the disappearances of those young men through the years?"

"It's a strong possibility." Hope leaped in Pressley's

chest at the thought they might have a concrete clue to follow rather than just shadows and speculation.

"The group was quite active in the sixties and seventies, but everyone around here thought they'd died out or moved away when the sightings stopped." She printed off several pages, the old laser printer whirring and clicking. "Back then, folks would see groups of women in white roaming the woods off Highway 365, especially around prom time. A lot of rumors about ghosts started circulating, and some of the townsfolk still swear those woods are haunted to this day."

"Ghosts don't exist," Jackson said firmly, though his hand unconsciously moved to touch the bandage on the back of his head.

"Oh, I know that perfectly well." The librarian smiled and retrieved the printed pages from the printer tray. "Demons, maybe, but not ghosts. Those so-called supernatural sightings were only women playing dress-up and perpetuating legends from the past, wearing white gowns and luring unsuspecting fools to their deaths. Here—this is all the documented information I have on the White Veil Society." She handed him the pages with the reverence of someone passing along historical treasure. "You can use that empty conference room over there if you want privacy while reading through them."

"Thank you so much for your help, Mrs. Patterson."

"My pleasure. I've always been fascinated by local

folklore, especially when it turns out to have a basis in reality."

Pressley followed Jackson to the small conference room, noting how the fluorescent lighting cast harsh shadows that seemed fitting given their subject matter. The symbols they'd photographed at the ritualistic clearing showed up clearly in several of the historical documents. There were even a few grainy black-and-white photographs from the 1960s showing women in white dresses dancing among the trees, their dark hair flowing as they moved in what looked like some kind of ceremony. All of them appeared to be young, and all had the same general appearance—dark hair, pale skin, slender builds.

She frowned and set the papers down on the conference table. "We need to look at missing persons reports and unsolved murders from other times of the year, not just prom season. I can't believe a group like this one only kills once a year, and I'm shocked the police haven't taken it more seriously over the decades. If they hate men as much as this suggests, then they hate all men, not just kindhearted teenagers willing to give a lone girl a ride."

Jackson nodded grimly as he studied a map showing historical sightings of the group. "We should go back to the woods and enter from the opposite direction this time. The forest covers a huge area— several hundred acres according to this. If this White Veil Society is still active, they have to have a permanent base of operations somewhere, not just a clearing with a fire pit."

She wanted to tell him again to let the authorities take over, to walk away before someone got seriously hurt or killed. If something happened to him in those dark woods, she wouldn't be able to protect him. Being a journalist turned private investigator didn't make her a trained fighter or tactical expert.

"Let's go investigate. Once we find out where they take their victims, we can give the location to Anderson and let his people handle the actual arrests."

"And then we'll walk away from this case?" she asked, hoping against hope that he'd finally agree to prioritize their safety.

He didn't answer directly but gathered up the papers with swift, efficient movements. "I bet they're using an abandoned cabin or house out there somewhere. Something far enough away from civilization that no one can hear their victims' screams or calls for help."

So he was avoiding her question, which meant he had no intention of backing down. She stormed after him back to the car, frustration and fear warring in her chest.

Jackson drove them to an old logging road that appeared on the historical maps Mrs. Patterson had provided. They bounced over potholes so deep they sent Pressley's head banging into the roof of the car despite her seatbelt, and loose gravel pinged against the undercarriage with sounds like gunshots.

"Sorry about the rough ride." Jackson shot her a quick, apologetic glance. "If I go any slower on this terrain, we might as well get out and walk. The car could get stuck in one of these holes."

"I understand the necessity." She grabbed the handle above her right shoulder and held on for dear life. "Do you actually know where we're going, or are we just driving blind through the wilderness?"

"If I read the historical survey map correctly, there should be an overgrown road branching off to our left somewhere up ahead. A road, even an unused one, usually means there were once people who lived out here. And people mean buildings that could still be standing."

Buildings that could provide dangerous people with perfect hiding places. Her heart lodged in her throat when Jackson stopped the car and pointed out a barely noticeable break in the tree line. A path so overgrown with weeds, saplings, and thick grass that she would have missed it entirely if he hadn't pointed it out.

Jackson popped the trunk and removed a collapsible shovel from their emergency kit, extending it to its full length with practiced efficiency.

Pressley slung her backpack over her shoulders, checking to make sure her phone was fully charged and her camera was easily accessible. She followed him down the path, noting how the vegetation seemed to close in around them as if the forest itself was trying to hide whatever lay ahead.

They'd traveled about the length of a football field through increasingly dense undergrowth when they stumbled into a clearing much larger than the ritualistic site from the day before. This one surrounded a cabin that didn't look nearly as abandoned as Pressley had expected. The structure had once been a gorgeous home—a two-story house with Victorian-era architectural details and a wraparound porch that must have been beautiful in its heyday. A separate wooden door to the side of the main porch most likely led to a root cellar or storm shelter, common features in homes built in this region during the early 1900s.

"Stay close to me," Jackson said quietly, propping the shovel against a nearby tree within easy reach. "It's possible someone friendly lives here and just values their privacy. Or it could be something much more sinister."

She tended to agree with his caution. The air around the cabin hung heavy and still, as if holding its breath while it waited to see what would transpire. Even the usual forest sounds—bird calls, rustling leaves, scurrying small animals—seemed muted here.

Jackson approached the front door with careful, measured steps and knocked firmly. When no one answered after a full minute, he tried the antique brass doorknob. The door opened easily at his touch, the hinges creaking softly in the silence. "Hello? Anyone home?" He glanced over his shoulder at Pressley, his expression troubled. "No one's here, or at least no one's answering."

"We can't just walk into someone's private home, Jackson."

"Who's going to know? And more importantly, who's going to stop us?"

"You used to be a police officer. You know about the Fourth Amendment and illegal search and seizure."

He frowned, but there was a hint of his old rebellious streak in his expression. "Used to be is the operative phrase. Now the Fourth Amendment doesn't apply to private investigators working a case. Besides, when did you suddenly decide to follow every rule in the book?"

When his life was threatened by unknown killers, that's when. She squared her shoulders and reluctantly followed him inside, every instinct screaming that they were making a terrible mistake.

Not a stick of furniture remained in the front room—just dust motes dancing in the shafts of sunlight that filtered through dirty windows. The kitchen cabinets stood open and empty, their doors hanging at odd angles. All three bedrooms upstairs were equally barren, showing no signs of recent habitation. Yet despite the apparent abandonment, the floors were surprisingly free of the thick layer of dust she would have expected, as if someone had been cleaning regularly.

"Let's check out that storm shelter," Jackson said, leading the way back outside.

A simple padlock kept the wooden door closed. He retrieved the shovel and slammed it against the lock repeatedly until the metal finally gave way and clattered to the ground.

Pressley swallowed against a suddenly dry throat and followed him down rough cement steps into the underground space. A single bare light bulb hanging from a frayed cord sprang to life when Jackson pulled the chain, casting harsh shadows on the concrete walls.

What they found made her blood run cold. In the center of the room sat a single wooden chair, its arms and legs stained dark with what could only be blood. Handcuffs hung from a nail driven into the wall, the metal worn smooth from repeated use. A small, rickety table held an assortment of knives in various sizes, their blades gleaming in the stark light. An ominous-looking chest sat against the opposite wall, its lid secured with a newer padlock. This was not a storm shelter. This was a carefully designed chamber of torture. She snapped pictures with her phone, her hands shaking so badly she could barely hold the device steady.

Her hands continued to tremble as she used a loose piece of metal to break open the chest's lock. Inside lay a horrifying collection of men's watches and jewelry, class rings, wallets, and even a few neckties. "Another collection of trophies from their victims."

"This dark stain around the chair—it's blood. A

very large amount of it." Jackson crouched near the chair, his face grim. "This is where the men were tortured and killed before their bodies were transported to the burial site."

"So, they're enticed to stop along the highway, then brought here to be brutalized before death." Pressley's heart ached at the suffering those young men must have endured, all for the simple crime of trying to help someone in need. "This house isn't particularly close to the Hensley place, is it? Why transport the bodies all that way for burial?"

"Let me check." He stepped back outside and put Mildred's address into his phone's GPS while Pressley watched over his shoulder, dreading what they might discover.

"We're less than half a mile away through the woods," he said quietly. "Much closer than I thought."

Still, why not bury the men closer to this torture chamber? Unless the women specifically wanted to bury their victims close to Lilly's resting place, as if they were making some offering to her memory. "The evil of this place makes the very air feel foul and contaminated."

"'Greater is He that is in me, than he who is of this world,'" Jackson quoted softly as he stared into the surrounding trees, his hand moving unconsciously to the cross he wore under his shirt.

Faint laughter drifted across the clearing from somewhere in the woods. The sound of multiple women's voices raised in what might have been amusement or celebration. Several figures in flowing white dresses darted between the trees at the edge of the clearing, visible for just moments before disappearing back into the shadows.

"Can we please go now?" Pressley grabbed his arm urgently, every survival instinct she possessed screaming at her to run.

"Absolutely." Jackson shielded her with his body as they ran back down the overgrown path as fast as the terrain would allow.

The White Veil Society was still active and operating in these woods. She doubted there would be any evidence left behind for the authorities by the time they could organize a proper search of the torture chamber, but at least she had the photographs on her phone as proof of what they'd discovered. She'd be surprised if the entire house was still standing when law enforcement finally arrived at the scene.

Back at the car, Jackson drove down the rutted logging road as fast as the deep holes and loose gravel would allow, bouncing them around like dice in a cup until Pressley's insides felt like a smoothie in a blender. He increased their speed dramatically when they hit the main logging road, then pushed the sedan to its limits on the highway, driving as if the hounds of hell were pursuing them.

"What was the shovel actually for?" she asked when she could finally speak without biting her tongue.

"In case I needed to do some excavating around the house. We didn't have time to scour the exterior grounds. I know when we're outnumbered and outgunned."

"They're specifically after you, Jackson. I'm just collateral damage in their eyes. We have to stop this investigation before it's too late."

"Not until we've finished what we started."

"We might not get the chance to finish! You'll end up dead like all those other men, and I'll be left to explain to your family why I let you walk into an obvious trap." Why wouldn't he listen to reason?

"We're too close to solving this to stop now." His face darkened with stubborn determination. "I've never quit anything in my life, and I'm not starting with this case."

"This isn't our fight anymore," she said through gritted teeth. "We found Ethan's body, which was what we were hired to do."

"You've said that before." His hands tightened on the steering wheel until his knuckles went white. "This discussion is over. If you want to quit, that's your prerogative, but I'm going to see this through to whatever end awaits."

God help them both, she thought desperately, before one of them ended up dead in those cursed woods.

Chapter Eight

Pressley listened to the answering machine and jotted down the name of the local cemetery, Whispering Oaks, in her careful handwriting. The red light blinked insistently as the gravelly voice of an older man filled their office. "We might have something promising. A man by the name of Benjamin Perry said some strange things have been going on at the cemetery that might be related to our case."

"Perry?" Jackson looked up from his computer, his eyebrows raised with interest.

"Son of the late Benjamin Perry, maybe." She grabbed her bag and checked that her phone was fully charged. "Let's go." Another lead, any lead, brought them one step closer to solving the mystery surrounding Lilly's death and the decades of murders that had followed.

The drive to Whispering Oaks Cemetery took them through the older part of town, where antebellum houses sat back from tree-lined streets and Spanish moss draped from ancient oaks like tattered funeral shrouds. The cemetery itself was surprisingly well-maintained, with manicured lawns and carefully tended flower beds that spoke of pride and reverence for the dead.

A middle-aged man with salt-and-pepper hair leaned heavily on a carved wooden cane when they arrived at the cemetery's main entrance. Despite his apparent need for the walking aid, he moved with purpose and dignity. "I've been reading about this case in the papers, and frankly, it's got me spooked. Guess you already know my father and Lilly were supposed to be married."

"Yes, sir." Pressley glanced around the well-cared-for cemetery, noting how peaceful it seemed in the afternoon sunlight. Marble angels watched over ornate headstones, and the sound of wind chimes created a gentle melody that should have been soothing but somehow felt ominous given their recent experiences. "We heard your father left town after Lilly's death."

"He did, but he always wanted to be buried in this town where he'd been happiest. I brought his body back here when he died, and I decided to stay and take care of the cemetery." His expression grew troubled. "My mother wasn't too happy about that decision, though."

"Why was that?" Pressley asked, sensing there was more to the story.

The man leaned against the wrought-iron railing in front of the cemetery office, his weathered hands gripping the cane tightly. "She said his love for Lilly had cursed our entire family. Said my father never got over his first love, that he spent his whole life pining for a dead woman instead of appreciating the living one he'd married." He shrugged, but Pressley could see the pain that still lingered in his eyes. "Maybe she was right. He talked about Lilly until the day he died, wondering what their life together would have been like. I'll show you his grave. It's where the really weird things have been happening lately."

They followed the man as he walked at a slow but steady gait through the cemetery, past elaborate Victorian monuments and simple granite markers that told the stories of lives lived and lost. The air hung heavy with the scent of magnolias and something else. Something that reminded Pressley of the funeral flowers they'd encountered in the woods. The silence was broken only by the occasional caw of crows perched in the towering oak trees and the distant sound of wind chimes carried on the breeze.

He led them up a brick path that had been swept meticulously clean, not a single leaf or twig marring its surface. "Here it is." Benjamin pointed to a well-maintained grave with a simple but elegant headstone bearing his father's name and dates.

Lying near the base of the tombstone was a single black rose, its petals so dark they seemed to absorb the light around them.

"A couple of times a week, an old woman comes and leaves one of these. I've tried talking to her once or twice, but she just glares at me with the most hateful expression I've ever seen and rushes off like she's afraid I might follow her."

Pressley's skin prickled with recognition. The description sounded exactly like what she'd expect from Mildred Hensley. "Can you describe this woman in more detail?"

"Always dressed head to toe in black with a heavy veil that completely hides her face. I know she's elderly from her gnarled hands and the way she moves—kind of shuffling and bent over. But there's something about her posture that suggests she's not as frail as she appears."

"All she does is leave the rose?" Jackson asked, crouching down to examine the flower without touching it.

"She mumbles something, but I've never been able to hear what she's saying. Sometimes, she looks like she's mourning, standing there with her head bowed like she's saying a prayer. Other times she seems angry, gesturing at the headstone like she's having an argument with my father's ghost."

"Why would she be angry with your father?" Pressley glanced around them, noting how isolated this section of the cemetery was from the main pathways.

"No idea whatsoever. The only woman I ever

knew to be angry with him was my mother, and she's been dead for ten years now."

"How did your father die, if you don't mind me asking?" Jackson straightened, his expression growing more serious.

Benjamin dusted off a weathered stone bench near the grave and sat down heavily, his cane resting across his knees. "He disappeared one night about fifteen years ago, and his body was found the next morning in a ditch about twenty miles from where he'd been staying. The authorities said he'd been murdered—beaten over the head with a blunt-force object multiple times, but they never found the murderer or even developed any solid leads."

Pressley exchanged a solemn look with Jackson. Another murder that hadn't been on their radar, another piece of the puzzle that seemed to connect to the larger pattern of violence surrounding this case.

"That ain't all, though." Benjamin pointed his cane toward the dense woods that bordered the back section of the cemetery. "On the nights when the old woman doesn't come to visit, I hear things. Whispers that seem to come from nowhere, laughter that doesn't sound quite human, the sound of running feet when there's no one around. At first, I thought it was just teenagers playing pranks. They do that sometimes, trying to scare each other in graveyards, but now I'm not so sure it's anything that innocent."

"Why don't you think it's kids anymore?" Pressley

took a step closer to Jackson, already dreading what Benjamin was going to say next based on their recent experiences.

"Because I've seen them with my own eyes. Women in flowing white dresses, dancing around the graves like they're performing some kind of ritual, flitting through the trees like supernatural beings. Maybe they're ghosts calling us to join them in death. I'm smart enough not to follow them, though. I've heard about all the other men who disappeared over the years and were never found."

"Why did you call us, Mr. Perry, instead of going to the police with this information?" Jackson asked, genuinely curious.

"As far as I can see, there's been no actual crime committed here at the cemetery. I don't have No Trespassing signs posted because I believe folks should be able to visit their loved ones any time they need to, day or night. I can't very well call the police just because of dancing ladies, now can I? They'd think I was some crazy old coot seeing things."

Pressley bent down and studied the black silk ribbon tied around the rose's stem. A small gold symbol identical to the ones they'd photographed in the ritualistic clearing had been pressed into the fabric—more evidence linking these incidents to the White Veil Society. Benjamin had encountered the women of The White Veil Society and lived to tell the tale, despite being male and alone in an isolated location.

"Which direction does this woman visitor go when she leaves?" Pressley asked, straightening up and scanning the tree line.

"She heads out through the back gate and disappears into the woods. There used to be a small chapel back there about half a mile down an old path, but it's been abandoned for decades and has probably fallen into complete ruin by now." He peered up at the two of them with eyes that held both concern and warning. "I've got one piece of advice for you both, and I hope you'll take it seriously. The dead don't stay quiet for long around here, and I have a feeling something big is about to happen."

"Thank you for calling us, Mr. Perry." Jackson took Pressley's hand in a gesture that was both protective and comforting. "Let's go see this abandoned chapel."

"You think it's significant to our case? The society's main rituals seemed to happen in that clearing near Mildred's property," she said, stepping up her pace to keep up with Jackson's longer stride as they headed toward the back of the cemetery.

"We're already here, so we might as well check it out thoroughly. Every piece of information could be important."

"I think the woman in black is Mildred," Pressley said with growing certainty.

"I completely agree with that assessment."

"But why would she mourn at the grave of a

man?" Pressley tugged him to a halt, genuinely puzzled by this behavior. "She seems to hate the entire male gender. Why show this kind of reverence for Benjamin Perry?"

"Benjamin Perry was the man her sister loved and planned to marry, not the man who killed her. Maybe he's the only man she doesn't actively despise because he represents what Lilly could have had if she'd lived."

She shrugged, considering the psychological implications. "That sounds like the twisted reasoning of someone who's mentally unstable and has been living with grief and rage for decades." They resumed their trek down a well-worn but narrow path that wound through increasingly dense vegetation. They'd been spending a lot of time in wooded areas lately—something she used to enjoy during her journalism days when she'd hike for relaxation. Now, the solitude and isolation of the forest left her feeling uneasy and exposed.

The chapel, when they finally reached it, was a heartbreaking sight. Blackened by fire and partially collapsed, it lay in a heap of scorched timbers and ash that spoke of violent destruction rather than simple abandonment. Shards of what had once been beautiful stained-glass windows glittered from the ground like scattered jewels, catching the afternoon sunlight in brief, colorful flashes. There hadn't been any church services or religious rituals held here for a very long time, that much was obvious.

The path continued past the ruined chapel, winding deeper into the woods. "Let's go a bit further and see where this leads," Jackson said, his investigative instincts engaged.

She stifled a groan but followed reluctantly. Why couldn't their investigation take place within the civilized city limits where there were streetlights and other people around? The path eventually led them to Highway 365, as everything connected to this case seemed to do. "We should pay Mildred another visit and confront her directly about what we've learned."

Jackson shook his head emphatically. "Mildred made it crystal clear that she'd shoot us if we came back to her property. Given what we now know about her potential involvement in multiple murders, she'd probably take aim at me first since I'm the male."

"Then we need to find someone who actually knew Tommy Raney personally. As Lilly's suspected killer, he might hold the key to understanding all of this violence. He supposedly disappeared right after her death, but we should check to see if he was one of the bodies that were dug up near Lilly's grave. If he wasn't among the victims, then what really happened to him?" Pressley paused, working through the implications. "Tommy might be the original reason those women developed such hatred for men. Maybe they started out seeking revenge against one specific killer, but now they lump the entire male species into the same category as rapists and murderers." Jackson included, which terrified her.

"My contact with the Texarkana Police Department might be able to give us some background information on the Raney family. I'll call him when we get back to the office. We're not going to find anything else useful out here in these woods."

Thank God, they were finally headed back to solid concrete under her feet, away from the ever-present threat of women in white emerging from the shadows.

Safely back at their office with its reassuring normalcy, Pressley ordered Chinese takeout from their favorite restaurant while Jackson contacted his friend in law enforcement. While she waited for both the food and the information, she mentally reviewed everything they knew so far, which still wasn't nearly enough to solve this case.

Tommy Raney allegedly kills Lilly Hensley just days before her scheduled wedding.

After that tragic event, young men began disappearing each year during prom season.

Additional evidence suggests men are being lured and killed throughout the year, not just during prom season.

An unidentified old woman regularly leaves black roses on Benjamin Perry's grave.

A society of women dressed in white appears to be responsible for the ongoing deaths, although the police have no concrete evidence to prove this theory.

Mildred Hensley seems to be connected to

everything, despite her claims of ignorance.

Pressley tapped a pencil rhythmically on her desk, a nervous habit that helped her think. Everything in this case circled back to Mildred Hensley like water spiraling down a drain. She had to have known about the bodies buried near Lilly's grave. You can't dig that many graves close to someone's house without them noticing. She had to have known about the women in white who roamed the nearby woods, and she may very well have been one of them herself during her younger days when she was physically capable of more strenuous activities.

What connection did the women in white have to Mildred Hensley? Were there other women in the community who had been hurt by men or had lost family members to male violence and now sought revenge? Was this some kind of twisted support group that had evolved into a murder cult?

"Got something promising." Jackson grinned as he hung up the phone, the first genuinely happy expression she'd seen from him in days. "Tommy Raney has a younger brother living in the Redwood nursing home on the other side of town."

"Is he mentally competent enough to give us useful information?"

"The nurse I spoke with said he's in the facility because a serious car accident left him permanently disabled and unable to care for himself, but his mind is still sharp as a tack. Let's finish eating this excellent

Chinese food and pay him a visit. He might be able to give us some real insight into Tommy's character and motivations, maybe even shed some light on why he would have killed Lilly."

The Redwood nursing home was a modern, well-maintained facility that smelled of disinfectant and had the kind of institutional cheerfulness that always made Pressley feel slightly depressed. Joseph Raney seemed genuinely happy to see them when they were escorted to the common room, but his smile faded quickly when they explained the purpose of their visit. Morbidly obese and confined to a motorized wheelchair, he needed an aide to help position him comfortably before they could begin their conversation.

"I don't get many visitors these days. This is a nice surprise, even if the subject matter isn't particularly pleasant." His voice was clear and strong despite his physical limitations.

Jackson introduced himself and Pressley to the elderly man, noting the sharp intelligence in his eyes. "We'd like to talk to you about your brother Tommy and the events surrounding Lilly Hensley's death."

"I haven't seen my brother since the day Lilly Hensley died, and that was over seventy years ago." Joseph frowned deeply, the wrinkles on his face deepening with the expression. "What could you possibly want to know about something that happened so many years ago? Most folks who were around then are dead and buried now."

"Do you believe Tommy actually killed Lilly?" Jackson leaned forward, his voice gentle but persistent.

Joseph shrugged his massive shoulders. "He could have, I suppose. My older brother was always a hothead, constantly in and out of trouble with the law for fighting and drinking. He liked Lilly something fierce and absolutely hated the fact that she was going to marry that Benjamin Perry fellow. But to actually rape and strangle her—" He shook his head slowly. "I just don't see Tommy doing something that vicious and brutal."

"Do you have any idea who else might have killed her? Why was Tommy considered the prime suspect by the authorities?"

"The police needed someone to pin the crime on, and since my brother conveniently disappeared right after her body was found, it made him look guilty as sin." Joseph smoothed a wrinkle on the blanket that covered his legs. "Someone claimed they overheard him talking to a friend about how if he couldn't have Lilly, then no one would be allowed to have her. But I think that was just talk, the kind of stupid thing young men say when they're drunk and heartbroken." He sighed heavily. "Like I said, he genuinely loved that girl. Guess we'll never know for sure who really killed her."

"No one else comes to mind as a potential suspect?" Pressley asked, hoping for any new leads.

"Lots of men in town loved Lilly Hensley. She

was the kind of girl who attracted attention wherever she went."

"Was she promiscuous?" Pressley asked delicately.

"Lord, no. She was actually quite sheltered and innocent. Sweet and kind to everyone she met, never had a harsh word for anybody. That's what made her so appealing. She was genuinely good-hearted." He heaved another sigh. "I've always thought it was probably just some vagrant passing through town who saw a pretty girl walking alone and took advantage of the opportunity. She'd been warned countless times not to walk that highway by herself, especially after dark."

They'd learned nothing new or particularly useful. "Are you aware of all the men's bodies that were recently found buried near Lilly's grave?"

He nodded grimly. "I watch the news religiously. Don't have much else to do in this place."

"What can you tell us about Mildred Hensley, Lilly's twin sister?"

Joseph's expression darkened considerably. "The complete opposite of her sister in every way that mattered. Mildred's as mean as a cornered copperhead and twice as venomous. Used to be a real beauty just like Lilly when they were young, but time, grief, and an obsessive desire for revenge turned her ugly inside and out."

"Revenge?" Pressley sat up straighter, sensing they were finally getting to something important.

"Oh, yes indeed. She came to see me personally right after Lilly's funeral, and I'll never forget the look in her eyes. Said she'd find Tommy wherever he was hiding and make him pay for what he'd done to her sister. Swore she'd hunt him down like a rabid dog." His gaze hardened with the memory. "For all I know, she found him and killed him before he could get very far out of town. You take a real good look at that woman if you get the chance. She's evil through and through, and she's had decades to let that evil fester and grow."

Chapter Nine

Jackson showed Pressley the DNA results on Amara, the laboratory report crisp and official-looking in its manila envelope. "She's a granddaughter to Mildred Hensley. The genetic markers are unmistakable."

"But Mildred specifically told us she didn't have any close relatives other than Lilly." Pressley crossed her arms and studied the results more carefully, noting the detailed breakdown of genetic relationships. Several additional names were listed as cousins to Amara—all women, all sharing significant DNA markers with the Hensley family line. Had they finally found the actual members of The White Veil Society hidden in plain sight within an extended family network?

"We both know she's a pathological liar. Here's the scientific proof of her deception." Jackson perched on the edge of her desk, his expression grim. "The question is how many more relatives are out there that we don't know about."

"I need to confront her directly with this evidence and force her to tell us the truth."

"Absolutely not." Jackson's voice carried the firm tone he'd used during his police days. "She specifically said she would shoot us if we came back, remember? That wasn't an idle threat."

"I think that was just a bluff designed to keep us away. If I go without you, she might be more willing to open up to me. I could play up to the whole hating-men angle, make her think I understand her perspective."

"You could die, Pressley. These people have killed dozens of men over the decades."

Better she risk her life than Jackson, given what they knew about the society's targeting preferences. Pressley met his concerned gaze steadily. "I won't die. Remember, I was the one who wanted to quit this investigation for safety reasons. You're the one who insisted we continue despite the obvious dangers. So now I'm going to talk to Mildred again and see how she responds to being caught in an outright lie." She stood decisively and grabbed her bag, checking to make sure her phone was fully charged. "If I'm not back within one hour, call Detective Anderson and send him to the Hensley place."

"Pressley..." His voice lowered to the intimate tone he used when he was truly worried about her.

"I love you more than my own life, Jackson, but I'm doing this, and you are not going with me." She kissed him tenderly, tasting the coffee on his lips and memorizing the feel of his arms around her. Then she marched determinedly out the door to her car, knowing that if she hesitated even for a moment, she'd lose her resolve. Her gaze met his through the office window as she backed away from the building, and she could see the worry etched on his face. She didn't like going against his wishes or causing him anxiety, but they needed to finish what they'd started if Jackson refused to quit the case. To accomplish that goal, she needed to speak to Mildred again without a threatening male presence by her side.

The drive to the Hensley property felt longer than usual, giving her too much time to second-guess her decision. By the time she arrived at the weathered old house, her heart had lodged firmly in her throat, and her hands were trembling slightly. She wiped sweaty palms on her dark slacks and slid out of the car, forcing herself to walk confidently toward the porch despite her internal fears.

Mildred stood waiting for her with arms crossed, glaring from her position on the front porch as if she'd been watching for Pressley's arrival. "Where's your sidekick? Finally come to your senses about trusting men?"

"We, uh, had a serious falling out about the direction of the investigation. Can we talk woman to woman?" Pressley tried to inject just the right note of frustration and disappointment into her voice.

Mildred stared at her for a long, calculating moment, her sharp blue eyes seeming to weigh Pressley's sincerity. Finally, she nodded curtly. "I just made some fresh coffee. Come inside where we can speak privately."

Pressley followed the older woman into the house, noting how the interior seemed even more cluttered and oppressive than during their previous visits. She sat carefully at a dinette set that looked like it could seat four people comfortably. Within seconds, a steaming cup of coffee sat in front of her, the liquid dark and aromatic. Mildred took the seat directly across the small table, her weathered hands wrapped around her cup.

"I know you didn't drive all the way out here just to vent about your partner troubles." The woman narrowed her eyes suspiciously. "What do you really want?"

"No, ma'am, I didn't come here for relationship advice." Pressley took the DNA results from her bag and slid them across the scratched wooden table. "These laboratory results suggest you had at least one child. Why did you lie to us about not having any close relatives?"

Mildred's face paled dramatically, the color draining from her cheeks as she stared at the official documents. "Because my daughter was a product of rape. Not exactly something a woman talks about freely, especially to strangers."

"Did you give her up for adoption?" Pressley

asked gently, trying to keep her tone non-judgmental.

"Of course not. It wasn't the innocent child's fault who her father was or how she came to be conceived. Instead, I kept her and raised her myself, teaching her to hate men the same way I'd learned to hate them."

"Except she didn't embrace that philosophy completely. Otherwise, there wouldn't be granddaughters and cousins listed in these genetic results."

Mildred's shoulders slumped in what looked like genuine defeat. "No, my daughter Millie decided to take a different approach with the male species. She chose to use men instead of simply avoiding them, coercing them with her body and feminine wiles to get whatever she wanted from them. She had one daughter out of wedlock, then two more with different fathers. Thus, all the granddaughters you've discovered."

Pressley leaned forward, resting her elbows on the table in a gesture of sympathy and shared confidence. "Who raped you, Mildred? Was it someone from town?"

"Tommy Raney. The same evil man who later assaulted and murdered my innocent sister Lilly."

Pressley swallowed hard against a suddenly dry mouth, then took a sip of the coffee to buy herself time to process this revelation. The liquid had a bitter aftertaste that seemed stronger than normal coffee. "Where is Tommy Raney now? Is he still alive?"

A sly, satisfied smile stretched across the older

woman's lips, transforming her face into something almost predatory. "I won't tell you that specific information. Just know with absolute certainty that you'll never find him, and he'll never hurt another woman again."

Tommy Raney must have been Mildred's very first victim, the catalyst that started her decades-long campaign of revenge. Pressley took another sip of the coffee, frowning as the bitter taste seemed to intensify. Her stomach suddenly dropped with a sickening realization. "What did you put in this coffee?"

"Nothing that will kill you outright." Mildred pushed to her feet with surprising agility for her age. "You'll just be a little incapacitated for a short while. No more than an hour or so. I'm going to put you somewhere safe in the attic until I can figure out exactly what to do with you."

"Are you planning to kill me?" Pressley's voice came out smaller than she'd intended.

"We don't kill women, as a general rule." Mildred hauled her to her unsteady feet and began dragging her toward a wooden ladder that led to an opening in the ceiling. The drug was already affecting Pressley's coordination, making her movements clumsy and uncertain. Once Mildred had shoved her through the opening into the dusty attic space, she slammed the trapdoor shut and Pressley heard the distinct sound of a lock being engaged. "I'll be back in a bit to check on you. Behave yourself and don't do anything foolish."

Pressley immediately stuck her finger down her throat, forcing herself to vomit up as much of the drugged coffee as possible. The bitter liquid burned her throat, but hopefully purging most of it would lessen the effects of whatever sedative Mildred had used. She reached instinctively for her cell phone, only to realize with growing panic that her bag was still downstairs in the kitchen, entirely out of reach.

She had no doubt that Jackson would come looking for her within the hour—probably sooner, knowing his protective instincts and tendency to worry. All she had to do was survive until then and try to gather whatever information she could while she was trapped. She sat heavily on an old steamer trunk, her legs feeling weak and unreliable. What an absolute idiot she'd been to come here alone, despite Jackson's warnings. In her arrogance, she'd thought she could handle Mildred, but she'd seriously underestimated the cunning and ruthlessness of the elderly woman.

Her arms hung heavy at her sides as she glanced around her makeshift prison, trying to assess her options. Cardboard boxes were stacked along the walls, covered in decades of dust and neglect. The floor was thick with grime and cobwebs. A small, round window sat high on one wall, potentially offering an escape route once her body started functioning normally again.

Sliding awkwardly to the floor, she managed to open the heavy trunk lid. Vintage clothes lay neatly folded inside—remnants of a time long gone, including what looked like dresses from the 1940s and 1950s. She pulled them out one by one with clumsy fingers, setting them carefully on a nearby box. At the very bottom of the trunk, wrapped in tissue paper, lay a white leather journal with "Lilly" etched elegantly into one corner.

Pressley's heart raced as she realized what she'd found. She crossed her legs as best she could and started to read with growing fascination and horror.

Dear Diary, Papa yelled at me again today for walking along the highway by myself. Why doesn't he understand that I'm waiting for someone special? Someone who makes my heart race just thinking about him.

Who was Lilly waiting for? If she was simply meeting her fiancé Benjamin, wouldn't she use his name in her private journal?

Dear Diary, He drove by again today and honked his horn at me. I almost jumped out of my skin with excitement. I swear I could hear him laughing as he passed by my walking spot. Why doesn't he ever stop to talk? I know he likes me. I can see it in his eyes when he looks at me. It can't be because I'm engaged to be married. He doesn't seem like the type to care about such conventional things. God will never forgive me for the sinful thoughts in my head about this man.

Pressley glanced at her watch, noting that she still had half an hour before Jackson would likely come looking for her. But she couldn't wait that long. She needed to get out of here immediately, before Mildred returned with reinforcements. She carefully buttoned the precious journal inside her shirt, then tottered unsteadily to the window, having to lean against the wall until the room stopped spinning so violently.

She constructed makeshift stairs out of the sturdier boxes and peered out the window into the afternoon sunlight. The drop looked manageable. She should be able to land on the slanted roof of the back porch, then jump down to the ground. If Mildred wasn't currently in the kitchen, Pressley could slip inside quickly, grab her bag, and escape before anyone noticed.

After saying a quick but fervent prayer for safety and asking for divine forgiveness for being such a fool, she managed to shimmy halfway out the narrow window on her stomach. She waited there for several long moments until the worst of the dizziness passed, then slid out the rest of the way, landing in an ungraceful heap on the tin roof of the back porch. The metal was hot from the sun and made alarming creaking sounds under her weight. She lay there motionless for a full minute, listening for any indication that Mildred had heard the commotion. When no one called out or came investigating, she carefully scooted to the edge of the roof, then dropped to the ground below.

A sharp cry of pain escaped her lips as her left ankle twisted on impact. The joint began to throb, and she realized there would be no running away from this situation. She'd have to move slowly and carefully.

She struggled to her feet, hissing against the intense pain shooting up her leg, and hobbled as quietly as possible to the back door. Through the window, she could see that the kitchen appeared to be empty. The door squeaked loudly as she opened it, and she held her breath, freezing in place and straining her ears for any sound. Again, no one called out or came to investigate.

Moving as fast as her injured ankle would allow, she entered the house and grabbed her bag from the floor near the chair where she'd been sitting. With a quick look around to make sure she wasn't being observed, she limped determinedly toward the front door. Her car beckoned from just a few yards away in the driveway. All she had to do was slip inside and drive away before Mildred returned, probably with white-dressed reinforcements from the society.

She fought back tears of pain and frustration as she hobbled toward her car, holding one arm tight across her chest so she didn't accidentally drop the journal. The secrets written in those pages could very well be what they needed to bring Mildred and her murderous society to justice.

Just as she reached for the car door handle, Mildred appeared around the corner of the house, moving with surprising speed for her age. The elderly woman carried a hunting rifle, and she aimed it at Pressley. So much for the claim about not killing women.

Pressley threw herself into the driver's seat and stomped on the gas pedal, crying out in agony as the movement sent fresh waves of pain through her injured ankle. Biting her lip hard enough to draw blood, she kept her foot pressed firmly on the accelerator and backed up rapidly, spinning dirt and gravel as she raced away from the house. Once she reached the safety of the highway, she immediately called Jackson using the Bluetooth system in her car.

"I'm on my way back to town." She tried to keep the pain and fear out of her voice. "I've got lots of important information to share with you."

"Thank God you're safe. I was just about to leave the office and come get you, despite your instructions."

"You would have missed me entirely. Can you meet me at the clinic instead of the office? I think I sprained my ankle pretty badly."

"Pressley—" His voice carried a mixture of relief and worry.

"I'm fine. Just banged up a bit. I'll see you there in a few minutes." She hung up and drove carefully to the medical clinic, trying not to put too much pressure on her injured ankle while operating the pedals.

Jackson arrived at the clinic only five minutes after she did, his face frantic with worry as he burst into the examination room where the nurse had positioned her. He wrapped his arms around her in a desperate embrace, then stepped back to press his forehead gently against hers. "Are you sure you're all right? When you said you were hurt—"

"I will be fine once these drugs work their way completely out of my system. I sprained my ankle climbing out of the attic window to escape."

He pulled up a chair and sat close to her, his expression a mixture of relief and exasperation. "You have some serious explaining to do, Pressley Taylor."

She told him everything. About the drugged coffee, being locked in the dusty attic, learning about Mildred's rape and secret child, finding Lilly's revealing journal, and finally escaping while Mildred shot at her with a rifle. "This journal is going to give us crucial evidence against The White Veil Society and their decades of crimes."

"But the society didn't exist when Lilly was originally killed, did it?"

"No, that's true. But they're certainly causing deadly havoc now, and we can prove it. We need to convince Anderson to put out an APB on Amara and probably several other women. Mildred might be the organizational leader, but she's far too old and frail to beat anyone to death with her bare hands. It takes a coordinated group of younger, stronger women to inflict the kind of massive physical damage that was done to Ethan."

"Are you finally on board to finish this

investigation properly?" He touched her cheek gently with the pad of his thumb.

"Yes, but we have to be smart about our approach from now on." She gripped his hand tightly. "You have to stay in the background during any confrontations, Jackson. Mildred specifically told me they don't kill women, which means you're in much more danger than I am."

"She shot at you with a rifle!" His face darkened with anger.

"And she deliberately missed. The drug she gave me was only meant to incapacitate me temporarily, not kill me outright. It wasn't supposed to last very long—just enough time for her to figure out what to do with me long-term. I think Mildred was probably planning to find a secure place to hold me until this entire situation resolved itself."

"Next time you might not be so lucky or resourceful."

"There absolutely won't be a next time." She'd learned the hard way that Mildred couldn't be trusted even slightly. The woman might be elderly, but her mind was razor-sharp and utterly without conscience.

No, it would be unwise to underestimate Mildred Hensley ever again.

Chapter Ten

Pressley yawned and glanced at the digital clock on her nightstand—twelve-thirty in the morning. She'd stayed up way past her usual bedtime reading Lilly's journal, completely absorbed in the tragic story that unfolded with each page. The handwriting was delicate and feminine, written with the careful penmanship that young women of the 1940s had been taught in school. She felt as if the story was unfolding right in front of her, as if she were watching the events play out in real time.

1947 Lilly

Dear Diary, Things are going to get bad. I can feel it in my bones, like a storm coming over the horizon. I've made such terrible choices, and now I don't know how to fix them...

Lilly paced in the ditch alongside the highway,

her heart racing with anticipation and dread in equal measure. She was hoping Tommy Raney would come by on his usual route home from working the rice fields. Over the past several weeks, he'd started stopping to spend time with her in the secluded woods, and those stolen moments had become the highlight of her otherwise predictable days.

She shouldn't be looking forward to seeing him with such desperate eagerness. Not after accepting Benjamin's proper marriage proposal in front of both their families, but the lure of a secret romance with the town's notorious bad boy was something she couldn't walk away from. The excitement that broke up her mundane, sheltered life, if only for an hour each day, wasn't something she was ready to give up. Not yet, anyway, but she knew she must. Today, she had to find the courage to tell Tommy goodbye forever.

Last night, under the cover of darkness and the old oak tree where they always met, Tommy had told her about his dreams beyond the confines of their small farming community—dreams of big cities, grand adventures, and a life far removed from the suffocating expectations of their conservative town. Dreams that prominently featured Lilly by his side. She couldn't allow him to keep thinking she would abandon everything and run away with him, no matter how tempting the prospect seemed in her weaker moments.

Her heart leaped with familiar excitement when she spotted his battered truck coming over the hill, dust trailing behind it like a wedding veil. She twisted her hands nervously in the folds of her best dress as he pulled off the road and stopped just a few feet from where she stood.

"There's my gorgeous girl," Tommy called out as he jumped from his truck with athletic grace. He ran to her and swept her into his strong arms, spinning her around until she was breathless with laughter. "Seeing you is the best part of my day, every day. Let's go to our special spot in the woods."

She knew she needed to say no, to end this dangerous liaison before it destroyed everything, but would one more time together really matter so much? Couldn't they spend some precious time together just once more before she broke his heart and her own in the process?

Hand in hand, they raced through the tall grass to the abandoned barn that had become their secret sanctuary. They threw themselves onto the old quilt she'd carefully spread across the hay-covered ground weeks ago during their first clandestine meeting. For this one stolen hour, she shoved aside all thoughts of dutiful Benjamin, of how God would surely view her sinful actions, and lost herself completely in Tommy's passionate kisses and tender caresses.

When their intimate encounter had reached its inevitable conclusion, rather than lying contentedly in his arms as she usually did, Lilly immediately pulled her dress back into its proper place and got to her feet with purpose. Through eyes brimming with unshed tears of regret and determination, she gazed down at Tommy's handsome, trusting face. She loved him with every fiber of her being, she truly did, but Benjamin could give her the secure, respectable life she'd been raised to want and expect.

"What's wrong, baby?" Tommy stretched a concerned hand out to her, his voice soft with post-intimacy tenderness.

Shaking her head slowly, she took a deliberate step backward, putting physical distance between them. "We can't do this anymore, Tommy. I'm so sorry for leading you on, but I'll always cherish the time we've spent together. However, I'm getting married to Benjamin after church on Sunday, just as planned."

His loving smile faded like a candle being snuffed out. "What exactly are you saying to me?"

"I'm saying goodbye, Tommy. For good this time."

He lunged to his feet so fast she didn't have time to blink before he grabbed her roughly and slammed her against the weathered barn wall. The splintered wood pricked through her dress and poked her bare arms, leaving tiny cuts that began to bleed.

"You're hurting me." She struggled to free herself from his iron grip.

"This is nothing compared to what I'm going to do if you insist on breaking up with me." His handsome face twisted with rage and betrayal.

"I have to marry Benjamin, Tommy. My family expects it, and it's the right thing to do." Her tears fell freely now, born of fear and pain as well as genuine sorrow.

He put his face so close to hers that his angry breath warmed her cheek. "I'll make your entire family sorry for this decision, Lilly. See if I don't." He slammed her against the wall again with vicious force, then repeated the action, before storming from the barn and leaving her alone with her terror and regret.

Sobbing uncontrollably, she wrapped her arms around her bruised middle and slid to the ground in despair. *Forgive me, God. I've made such a terrible mess of things. All because I wanted some excitement in my boring life.*

Night had fallen before she finally gathered the courage to leave the barn and make her way home through the darkness. When she approached the house, she found her older sister Mildred leaning against the wall of the porch, hunched over as if in severe pain. Her dress hung torn from one shoulder, exposing her undergarments, and her hair was disheveled.

"Millie?" Lilly rushed to her sister's side. "What's wrong? Are you hurt? What happened to you?"

Her sister snapped upright at the sound of her voice, eyes flashing with pain and fury. "Tommy did this to me! He assaulted me, Lilly. Took my virtue by force. All because of you, he said. He kept saying your name while he..." She couldn't finish the sentence. "Oh,

Lilly, what did you do to make him so angry?"

Lilly gasped and stumbled backward, horrified by the implications. What had she done indeed? Her parents could never know how much their supposedly sweet youngest child had fallen into sin and caused such terrible consequences. "We can't tell anyone about any of this. This has to be our secret forever. I'll take care of everything somehow."

"The damage has already been done to both of us. No decent man will have me now, not after this."

"Of course they will. A man who truly loves you will understand that it wasn't your fault." But even as she said the words, Lilly wondered if they were true. Would Benjamin forgive her for betraying him if he ever found out about her affair? She covered her face with her hands in shame. "I'm so sorry, Millie. This is all my fault."

"You should be sorry." Mildred shook her roughly. "You're right about keeping this secret. We won't talk of it again with anyone. We'll forget all about it and pray that neither one of us carries that evil man's seed."

"Oh, God." The possibility of pregnancy hadn't even occurred to Lilly until that moment. She put a protective hand to her stomach. If she did carry Tommy's child, she could pass it off as Benjamin's after they were married. It would be easy enough to manage.

"I can see your devious little mind working, Lillianne. No more lies. No more secrets after tonight."

"Girls? It's past time to eat supper. What are you doing out there?" Their mother called from the front door, her voice carrying a note of impatience.

"Just sister talk, Momma," Mildred replied. "We forgot about the time."

"Well, get in here right now. You shouldn't keep your father waiting for his meal. You know how he gets when he's been drinking."

Yes, they both knew all too well. By now, Papa would be well into his third or fourth beer of the evening and angry as a wet rooster that his supper was late. Momma would be the one to suffer his violent wrath, as she always did when things didn't go according to his expectations.

They ate supper in tense silence, the weight of their shared secret hanging over the table like a funeral shroud. When Papa finished eating, he narrowed his bloodshot eyes at Mildred suspiciously. "What have you done to your dress, girl?"

"I caught it on a piece of barbed wire while I was walking, Papa." She kept her gaze fixed firmly on her plate.

"And you, Lilly. You have straw in your hair like you've been rolling around in a barn. Have my girls been behaving improperly? If so, I'll take a switch to both of you until you can't sit down."

"No, Papa," they said in perfect unison, their voices small with fear.

"Don't lie to me. God sees all, and the truth will

always be revealed eventually." He pushed away from the table and returned to his radio, dismissing them.

Relieved that he'd left them alone, Lilly helped clear the table before gratefully going to bed, emotionally and physically exhausted.

Dear Diary, Tommy did the unthinkable to poor Millie, all because of my selfish actions. Somehow, I have to make things right before something else terrible happens to our family.

Just as her eyes were finally closing in sleep, a soft tapping sounded at her bedroom window. She padded across the cold floor to see Tommy standing in the moonlight below.

She thrust open the window and immediately smelled the alcohol on him. "You're drunk." She waved a hand in front of her face to ward off the fumes.

"Come out here right now. I want to speak to you." His words slurred together.

She glanced over to where Mildred was sleeping, snoring softly in her exhaustion. "Hush, you'll wake everyone. I'll be right there." She had to make him see reason and convince him to stay away from their family forever. If not for the fact that Papa would literally kill Tommy for what he'd done to Mildred, she'd spill everything and let her father handle the situation. But she had enough sins to account for when she faced God someday.

When she joined Tommy outside, still in her nightgown, he roughly gripped her arm and dragged her into the dark woods behind the house. In the shadows beneath the trees, he begged her desperately to call off the wedding and run away with him to start a new life somewhere far from Arkansas.

She yanked her arm free from his grip. "After what you did to my innocent sister tonight? You're even worse than what everyone in town says about you. I'm marrying Benjamin on Sunday as planned. Get used to the idea and leave us alone."

"Then Benjamin can't have you either," he snarled. His vicious punch knocked her to the ground, stunning her. He straddled her prone form, wrapping his large hands around her delicate throat.

She kicked and thrashed frantically, struggling to breathe as his grip tightened, until her world gradually went dark and silent.

~

Pressley rubbed the sleep from her tired eyes and turned the page of the diary with trembling fingers. The handwriting changed completely. This was different penmanship, more angular and desperate. She read on with growing horror.

1947 Mildred

Dear Diary, Things couldn't possibly be any worse than they are right now...

Didn't Lilly learn anything from what had happened earlier that evening? Mildred tossed aside her covers after noticing her sister's bed was empty, the sheets still warm but abandoned. Since the sun had just started to rise over the horizon, casting long shadows across their shared bedroom, Lilly must have snuck out sometime during the night hours. So why wasn't she home yet? Something felt wrong.

She climbed carefully out the window and headed for the highway—the place Lilly always went when she was troubled or excited. Now Mildred knew exactly why her sister was drawn to that lonely stretch of road. She went there to meet Tommy Raney in secret.

She kept to the shadows along the tree line in case one of her parents happened to glance out a window and spot her wandering around in her nightgown. When she finally reached the highway, Mildred froze in absolute horror at the sight before her. Tommy dragged her sister's limp form into the deep ditch beside the road. Lilly didn't move at all, couldn't move. Her sightless eyes stared toward heaven, and the white of her nightgown created a stark, ghostly contrast against the dark ground she lay upon.

Rage filled Mildred like a living thing, hot and consuming. She grabbed the closest weapon she could find—a fallen tree branch as thick around as her wrist and heavy with the weight of dense wood. Without another coherent thought beyond the need for justice, she sprinted forward and brought it down hard on

Tommy's skull with all her strength. She struck again and again, her fury giving her supernatural power, until her physical strength finally gave out and Tommy lay motionless beside her murdered sister.

She tossed the bloodied branch deep into the trees and grabbed Tommy's ankles with grim determination. No way would she allow him to lie beside her dear sister in death. He didn't deserve that honor. She knew exactly what to do with human garbage. Dragging his body was backbreaking work, and before she reached Henderson's hog farm a mile away, she almost gave up from exhaustion. But she forced herself to continue, driven by love for Lilly and hatred for her killer. Once there, she rolled his body under the fence and left him for the hogs to dispose of, knowing they would consume every trace of evidence.

Then she went home to face the devastating grief that would fill their house once Papa discovered Lilly's body on his way to work at the lumber mill, as she knew he inevitably would.

That was the final entry in the diary. Tears coursed down Pressley's cheeks as she closed the precious book with reverent hands.

The answer as to what had happened between Lilly, Tommy, and Mildred had finally been revealed in the most tragic way possible. The question remained whether the child Mildred had borne years later had been Tommy's or some other man's. Given that the fateful day of her sister's brutal death had soured

Mildred permanently on the entire male gender, Pressley felt certain the child had indeed been Tommy's, conceived during that violent assault.

So much pain and destruction because a sheltered young girl had been lured by the dangerous charms of the town's notorious bad boy. Pressley clutched the diary to her chest and stared at the ceiling of her bedroom, processing the full implications of what she'd learned. While Lilly's own words had answered some crucial questions, they still needed concrete confirmation that Mildred and her extensive network of female relatives were responsible for the systematic deaths of all those innocent young men over the decades.

How could she and Jackson prove it without serious harm coming to him in the process?

The next morning, the profound sadness from reading the journal still filled her heart as she mechanically went through the motions of making coffee. The tragic story had affected her more deeply than she'd expected, and she found herself thinking about how different things might have been if Lilly had made other choices.

When Jackson entered the office right on schedule, he took one look at her face and immediately asked what was wrong, his voice filled with concern.

She told him everything she'd read in careful detail, sharing the heartbreaking story of love, betrayal, assault, and murder. "It's such a tragic story of how one bad decision can destroy so many lives."

"Life is often tragic in ways we never expect," he said solemnly, accepting the cup of coffee she offered him. "There's been far too much death over the years in this town, but we're going to put an end to a significant portion of it. I can feel that we're getting close to solving this."

Legal justice might not have been done for Lilly all those decades ago, but they could help make it right for Ethan and all the other innocent men who had died since then. "Since I've finished reading the entire journal, we can turn it over to Anderson as evidence and let him know about Mildred drugging and imprisoning me in her attic. He'll at least be able to drag her in for official questioning."

"I seriously doubt he'll be able to make any arrests based on what we have," Jackson said thoughtfully. "She'll simply claim you were trespassing on her private property, and she feared for her safety. She might even say she locked you up temporarily so she could call the police to come and arrest you for breaking and entering."

"But she shot at me with a rifle."

"Again, you were trespassing on posted property after she'd explicitly warned us what would happen if we set foot there again. She could claim she was firing warning shots."

"That's probably true," she sighed, taking her coffee to her desk and settling into her chair. "I don't know how to prove that Mildred killed Tommy Raney all those years ago, or that she's been orchestrating the deaths of all those other men since then. At least now I understand why Lilly didn't attend the prom—she was getting married two days later."

"Or perhaps her family was simply too poor to afford a fancy party dress and all the associated expenses," Jackson pointed out. "Whether she attended the prom or not has no bearing on her death. What matters is that her murder happened on prom night, which established the pattern."

And so had dozens of others since then. Pressley wrapped her hands around the hot mug in front of her, drawing comfort from its warmth. There had to be some way to catch the women responsible for these ongoing crimes without waiting until next year's prom season rolled around. But how could they accomplish that without putting Jackson in mortal danger?

Chapter Eleven

The door jingled cheerfully the next morning, a sound that seemed incongruous with the dark nature of their recent investigations. A young woman carrying an armload of colorful fliers entered the office, her bright smile suggesting she was excited about whatever she was promoting. She looked to be in her early twenties, with blonde hair pulled back in a ponytail and the kind of enthusiastic energy that marked her as either a college student or recent graduate.

"Can I put one of these in your window?" she asked, holding up one of the fliers. "It'll only take a second."

"Let me see it first." Pressley held out her hand, curious about what could warrant such widespread distribution. Her frown deepened as she studied a professionally designed flier advertising something called "The Haunted Town of Redwood - A Spooky Weekend Festival." The graphics included dramatic images of ghostly figures and gothic lettering that would have been impressive if the subject matter weren't so inappropriate given current circumstances. "What exactly is this supposed to be?"

"Oh, it's so exciting! The town is holding a special festival this weekend to attract tourists from all over Arkansas and the surrounding states. By now, everyone within a hundred miles has heard about The Prom Night Hitchhiker legend. You know that poor girl who died way back in the 1940s?" The girl shrugged with the casual indifference of youth. "Lots of folks say her ghost haunts the old highway and lures unsuspecting men to their doom. The town council figured, why not capitalize on it and bring in some much-needed revenue?"

Because it would directly interfere with an ongoing murder investigation, for one thing. And because it was in spectacularly poor taste, for another. Pressley handed the flier to Jackson with a look of disgust. "You need to see this travesty."

"That is the dumbest thing I've seen in a very long time." He thrust the flier back at the girl with barely concealed irritation. "Go ahead and hang it up in our window if you must. It's not your fault this town is acting foolish and insensitive."

"There's, uh, a town meeting scheduled in the park this morning at eleven if you want to attend and voice your concerns." The girl quickly taped the flier to the front window and rushed out of the office, apparently sensing the tension in the room.

"We should probably attend that meeting so we know exactly what we're dealing with," Pressley suggested, already dreading what they might discover.

"First, we should see what Detective Anderson thinks about this upcoming festival and whether he's aware of the potential complications it could create." Jackson grabbed his car keys from his desk drawer. "This could seriously compromise the investigation."

At the police station, Anderson sat behind his desk, looking harried and drinking what appeared to be his fourth cup of coffee of the morning. He admitted to already knowing about the upcoming festival, though his expression suggested he was no happier about it than they were. "I'm hoping that Mildred or Amara will show up at some point during the festivities. After all, they have a huge personal stake in what happens in this town, especially now that I've read the deceased Lilly's journal and understand the full scope of their motivations." He crossed his arms and leaned back in his chair. "I sent Officer Martinez out to the Hensley place first thing this morning to bring Mildred in for official questioning. There was no sign of her anywhere on the property."

"Do you think she's skipped town entirely?" Pressley asked, though she suspected the answer wouldn't be that simple.

"It's possible, but I doubt it. This is her territory, her hunting ground. She's not going to abandon it easily." Anderson's expression grew more serious. "We'll keep our eyes open for both women. If either of you sees them, do not under any circumstances approach them. Call this office immediately, and we'll handle the apprehension. Is that understood?" He fixed Pressley with a particularly sharp gaze. "I don't care what that old woman told you about not killing women. She might make an exception in your case, especially since you've been getting so close to exposing her operation."

"Jackson is in far more danger than I am, but I appreciate your concern for my safety." She marched from the office, her irritation evident in every step.

"Why exactly did you tell him about Mildred locking me up in her attic?" She whirled to face Jackson as soon as he joined her outside the building. "I specifically asked you not to involve the police in that incident."

"Because it's one more criminal charge on that woman's rapidly growing list of offenses." He put his hand on the small of her back in a gesture that was both protective and calming. "I'm not going to apologize for caring about what happens to you and wanting to see her held accountable."

"You shouldn't have gone behind my back like that."

"Like you aren't constantly doing things behind mine that you think will keep me safe?" He arched a knowing brow. "We both know you've been making decisions based on protecting me rather than solving this case efficiently."

She didn't answer immediately, instead increasing her pace to the car while she processed his words. Inside the vehicle, she clicked on her seatbelt and stared out the window at the ordinary suburban street. Why was she upset that Jackson wanted the same level of protection for her that she desperately wanted for him? They were partners in every sense of the word, after all. They should have each other's backs without question.

A surprisingly large crowd had gathered at the municipal park by the time they arrived. The weather was perfect for an outdoor meeting—clear skies, comfortable temperature, and a gentle breeze that carried the scent of blooming dogwood trees. But the atmosphere among the assembled townspeople was anything but peaceful.

"The woman stepping up to the microphone in the gazebo is Karen Morrison," Jackson said, pointing toward a well-dressed blonde woman who appeared to be in her forties. "She owns the Redwood Inn, a bed and breakfast that's been struggling financially for the past couple of years. The man beside her is Brian Steele, an entrepreneur who's relatively new to town— arrived about six months ago with big plans for development."

"Both of whom would benefit significantly from a boost in tourism revenue. How do you know so much about the local business community?"

"I maintain a comprehensive computer file on all Redwood business owners and newcomers to the area. The real estate agent keeps me informed of new home purchases and rental agreements." He grinned with obvious pride in his thoroughness. "I'm a smart man who believes in being prepared."

"Smart aleck is more like it." She could never stay mad at him for long, especially when he was being genuinely helpful.

The owner of the bed and breakfast launched into what could only be described as a sales pitch, droning on and on about how playing up the story of their town being haunted would help Redwood economically during these difficult times. She spoke of increased hotel bookings, restaurant revenues, and retail sales with the enthusiasm of someone who saw dollar signs dancing in her head.

Her presentation was interrupted when an elderly man in the back of the crowd yelled out his objection.

"Hogwash! Complete and utter nonsense! We all know about that White Veil Society and what they really do. They kill men, plain and simple. Tourists won't be any safer than we locals are, and you're going to have blood on your hands when someone gets hurt."

Karen Morrison's face flushed with irritation as she glowered in the direction of the dissenting voice. "Hank, we also know from decades of evidence that the murders only happen on prom night. The police have already committed to shutting down Highway 365 every prom night in the future as a precautionary measure. This town desperately needs the income that tourism could provide."

"I lost my baby brother to those witches thirty years ago," an older woman called out, waving her walking cane for emphasis. "They're evil, and they're still out there somewhere."

"I'm very sorry for your loss, Betty, truly I am." Karen's tone softened slightly, though her determination remained evident. "But we can't let fear paralyze us forever. We need to move forward and find ways to support our community economically."

She turned back to address the portion of the group who seemed more receptive to the festival idea, but her presentation was interrupted again by a voice from the very back of the crowd.

"Bringing in outsiders will unearth secrets that are best left buried forever," the voice said ominously.

Pressley strained to see who had spoken, standing on her tiptoes and craning her neck. The voice belonged to a woman, probably younger than Karen or Betty, but she couldn't get a clear view through the crowd. "Can you see who that is?"

"No, too many people in the way." Jackson peered over the heads of the crowd, using his height advantage. "But whoever it was sounded like she knows something significant."

"I want to get the names of everyone who's opposing this festival and speak to them individually."

Starting with Betty, who had mentioned losing her brother. She grabbed Jackson's hand and pulled him through the crowd. "Ma'am? Excuse me?"

The elderly woman turned at the sound of Pressley's voice. "Yes, dear?"

Pressley quickly introduced herself and Jackson, noting that Betty's eyes showed the sharp intelligence of someone whose mind remained clear despite her advanced age. "We're helping the local police investigate the murder of Ethan Duvall and all the men who were killed before him. Did I hear you correctly when you said you lost your brother?"

"That's right. Prom night, forty years ago this spring." She tapped her wooden cane emphatically on the ground. "Those responsible are still out there somewhere, probably recruiting new members to their twisted cause. I think their group has been growing over the years, and bringing in a bunch of unsuspecting outsiders is going to significantly increase the danger. Who's to say they'll continue sticking to their tradition of only killing on prom night? The White Veil Society will suddenly have a whole new batch of potential male victims to target. It might be too much of a temptation for those man-killers to resist."

"Have you taken your concerns to the police over the years?"

"Sure have, many times. They always told me not to fabricate wild stories and to leave police work to the professionals." She tapped her cane harder against the ground, her frustration evident. "They've been no help whatsoever. Never have been, not in forty years of asking for justice. The authorities in this town have always preferred to sweep these murders under the rug rather than deal with them properly."

"Would you mind helping me over to that bench?" Jackson asked gently. "I'd like to ask you a few more questions if you're willing to share your knowledge."

"Of course, young man. You seem like decent folk, unlike some people in this town." Jackson carefully linked his arm with hers and helped her navigate to a nearby park bench.

"Do you know anyone else who might be able to answer questions about The White Veil Society or provide useful information?"

"Not really, unfortunately. Some people insist the group is nothing more than local legend, folklore that's gotten blown out of proportion over the decades. I say they're dead wrong, but no one listens to the ramblings of an old woman." She settled onto the bench with a grateful sigh. "My advice is to be very careful about who you trust in this town. Not everyone is who they appear to be."

"Do you know Mildred Hensley personally?" Pressley sat beside her on the weathered wooden bench.

"Oh, that hateful woman. She wasn't particularly kind to people even before the death of her sister, but she only got worse and more bitter afterward. I've always suspected she's somehow behind these deaths, but the authorities never could dig up any concrete evidence to support that theory." Betty's expression grew thoughtful. "I think you should spend some time going through the old newspaper archives housed in the library basement. Not all of the historical records have been scanned into the computer systems yet. When you review them chronologically, you'll see exactly how poorly these investigations have been conducted through the years."

"You two are the private investigators everyone's been talking about, right?" The voice came from directly behind the bench, causing all three of them to turn.

Brian Steele stood there with his arms crossed and his eyes narrowed in what could only be described as a threatening manner. He was a man in his thirties with the kind of aggressive confidence that often accompanied new money and big ambitions.

Jackson slowly stood and faced the newcomer. "That's right. Is there something we can help you with?"

"Don't mess up what could be a very good thing for this community," Steele said, his voice carrying an unmistakable warning.

"Or what exactly?" Jackson's tone remained calm, but Pressley could see the tension in his shoulders.

"This town desperately needs the tourist revenue that a successful festival could generate. We can't afford to let superstition and old wives' tales interfere with economic progress."

"You need the money badly enough to risk people's lives?"

The man's smirk was both condescending and infuriating. "Don't tell me you believe these ridiculous stories about a man-hating group of women roaming the woods? Those men who died over the years were killed by a transient serial killer who passes through town around the same time every year. I bet if you did some proper research, you'd find similar deaths in other communities along his route during different times of the year."

Jackson tilted his head, studying Steele's face carefully. "Do you have any facts or evidence to support that rather convenient theory?"

"It makes perfect logical sense to me, which is more than I can say for ghost stories and revenge cults." His gaze shifted to include both investigators. "I'm just telling you two not to mess this up for hardworking people who are trying to make a decent living. This festival could be the beginning of a real economic turnaround for Redwood."

He nodded curtly at Betty, then turned and walked back toward the gazebo where the debate was continuing with increasing volume.

"Arrogant idiot," Betty muttered, pushing herself to her feet with the help of her cane. "I've had quite enough excitement for one day. Good luck to both of you, and please be careful. This town has more secrets than most people realize."

She hobbled away, leaving Pressley and Jackson to watch as the festival discussion deteriorated into shouting matches between opposing factions. The divide in the community was deeper than simple disagreement about tourism strategy.

Karen Morrison grabbed a battery-powered bullhorn from somewhere in the gazebo and raised it to her lips. "Listen up, everyone! I've just received word that the mayor has officially approved this festival for next weekend. If you aren't happy with that decision, then don't attend, but I'm sure those of you with local businesses will appreciate the extra income it could generate. Remember, if you want to set up a vendor booth or participate in any way, please contact me as soon as possible. We have a tremendous amount of work to accomplish in just one week. This meeting is now officially adjourned."

"Do you think the women in white will change their pattern and target someone from the festival?" Pressley asked as they walked back toward their car.

"To what purpose would they break with decades of tradition? Their pattern of killing on prom night seems to be making a very specific statement. Their ongoing attempt to right what they see as a historical wrong from decades ago." Jackson took her hand and led her through the dispersing crowd. "Let's visit those newspaper archives Betty mentioned. I doubt we'll discover any groundbreaking new information, but we need to follow up on every potential lead, no matter how small."

"I agree." She didn't think the women in white would strike during the festival either, but it helped to hear that Jackson shared her assessment. There had already been far too much death and violence since Lilly's original murder.

The librarian, Mrs. Patterson, was more than happy to help them again and led them down a narrow staircase to a basement filled with dozens of labeled storage boxes. The air was musty and thick with the smell of old paper and dust. "I've done my absolute best to keep everything organized by year and general content, though I'm sure some things have been misfiled over the decades. I'll be at my desk upstairs if you need any assistance."

"Thank you so much for your help," Jackson said, already scanning the box labels. He took down a heavy cardboard box from the year Lilly was murdered and handed the newspapers from May 1947 to Pressley. "I don't think we'll find anything relevant before this specific date."

"No, probably not." She settled into a rickety wooden chair that had seen better days and began systematically skimming through the yellowed pages. She'd learned valuable information through old newspapers during their investigation of The Phantom case in Texarkana. Hopefully, they'd uncover something equally helpful this time.

After more than an hour of careful reading, all

they'd discovered were brief mentions of the prom night murders that provided little more than the identities of the deceased and the standard statement that there were no suspects or significant leads. "We need to track down and speak to one of the police officers who worked during those early years," Pressley said, stretching her cramped neck. "I want to find out why murders rated such small mentions in the local papers. They devoted more column space to church socials and community bake sales than to violent deaths."

Jackson placed the first box back on its designated shelf and retrieved another one from a different year. "I'm finding exactly the same pattern in later years. The coverage is consistently minimal and uninformative. Is it possible that one of the women involved in this 'Society' had some connection to law enforcement or the newspaper?"

"Not in the early years, anyway. Women weren't allowed to work as police officers or newspaper reporters back in the 1940s and 1950s. Although..." She paused, considering another possibility. "You don't think the men in town were simply scared to investigate too thoroughly, do you? Since a murder took place every single year around the same time, maybe journalists and police officers thought that asking too many questions would put targets on their backs. It seems far-fetched, but given the pattern, maybe they preferred to keep their heads down and hope someone else would eventually solve the problem."

"It could also just be plain incompetence or deliberate cover-up," Jackson suggested. "Downplaying the yearly murders could be as simple as local authorities not wanting the general public to panic. Remember, those were simpler times when people didn't expect the same level of transparency from their government officials. Small towns especially didn't like having their reputations tarnished by scandal."

She skimmed through another stack of newspapers, looking for any mention of the investigations or unusual details about the crimes. "Here's something interesting. Mildred's name is specifically mentioned in this article from the year after Lilly's death. The reporter interviewed her because she lived in one of only two houses along that stretch of Highway 365. She was quoted as saying that a young man had come to her house looking for the young lady he'd given a ride to, and she'd shown him Lilly's grave. This is almost exactly what she told us during our first visit."

"A well-rehearsed response that she's been perfecting for decades," Jackson observed. He unfolded the next newspaper in the chronological sequence. "Look at this—the following year she's quoted as saying virtually the same thing, almost word for word. I think Mildred has been purposefully building and maintaining this ghost story legend."

"As a way to deflect attention from what's happening around her property?"

"Exactly. Create a supernatural explanation that

people will either dismiss as nonsense or accept as something beyond human control." He leaned his elbows on the scarred wooden table and met her gaze directly. "Pressley, I know you're not going to like what I'm about to suggest, but I think we're going to have to set some kind of trap to catch these women in the act."

"Absolutely not. No way. Let Anderson set a trap if he thinks one is necessary, but I won't have you used as bait."

"He seems to be following in the footsteps of local law enforcement through the years—putting the deaths of all those young men on the back burner because he has other priorities. It's a small police force with limited resources, Pressley. They don't have the manpower or expertise to handle this kind of complex investigation."

"Then why hasn't the FBI been called in before now? It's obvious there's been a serial killer operating in and around Redwood for decades. Don't you still have contacts in the bureau from your police days?"

"Yes, I do have some connections. Anderson won't be happy about me going over his head and involving federal authorities, but I'll contact them as soon as we get back to the office. We're not going to find anything more useful down here."

"I completely agree." They carefully returned the newspaper boxes to their proper places on the shelves and headed back upstairs to the main library.

Back at their office, Pressley took a seat at her desk while Jackson made the important phone call to his FBI contact. When he finally hung up after a lengthy conversation, he looked up at her with an expression of relief.

"They were already planning to send a team to investigate after the discovery of all those bodies near Lilly's grave made the national news. The bureau has been monitoring the situation, and they'll have agents here by tomorrow morning."

She breathed a deep sigh of relief, feeling as if a tremendous weight had been lifted from her shoulders. The FBI's involvement would help ensure that Jackson stayed out of the deadly clutches of the women in white, and their resources would finally bring this decades-long nightmare to an end.

Chapter Twelve

Pressley stared at the open door to their office, her stomach dropping at the sight before her. The normally organized workspace looked like a tornado had torn through it with malicious intent. Papers were strewn across both desks and scattered across the floor like confetti, chairs were overturned and tossed carelessly aside, and drawers had been yanked out and their contents dumped everywhere. Both laptops and their external hard drives were completely gone, along with several case files that had been stored in the filing cabinet.

"We locked it when we left last night, didn't we?" She always made sure to secure the office before going upstairs to her apartment for the evening. The routine was so ingrained that she rarely even thought about it anymore. "Why didn't the alarm system sound? It should have been triggered the moment someone opened that door."

Jackson rushed outside to examine the building's exterior, returning a couple of minutes later with his jaw clenched in anger. "Someone cut the electrical cords to the entire alarm system. They knew exactly what they were doing." He moved to the wall near the door and pulled a sheet of paper that had been tacked there with what appeared to be a hunting knife. The blade had been driven so deep into the drywall that it took considerable effort to remove it. "They were considerate enough to leave us a message. It says to drop the case immediately. This is supposedly our last warning."

Heaving a frustrated sigh, Pressley began taking systematic pictures of the destruction with her cell phone, documenting the damage from multiple angles for insurance purposes and potential evidence. "Would you mind calling Anderson? This makes one more criminal incident to report, and I have a feeling this won't be the last."

"No need to make that call. They're already here." He jerked his head toward the parking lot where a squad car and a sleek black SUV were pulling into their assigned spaces.

"Good to see you again, Jackson." A tall, elegant Black woman dressed in a crisp dark suit approached them with a confident smile. Her professional demeanor and the way she carried herself immediately marked her as federal law enforcement.

"Victoria." He nodded toward her with a carefully

neutral expression, his face remaining grim despite her obvious pleasure at seeing him. "I honestly didn't expect them to send you specifically."

"When I saw that the request for federal assistance came directly from you, I volunteered to take point on this investigation. Old times' sake, you might say."

Pressley cleared her throat and offered her hand in greeting, though something about the woman's familiarity with Jackson made her uncomfortable. "I'm Pressley Taylor, Jackson's partner." She shot him a meaningful glance. He'd never mentioned this particular woman before, despite the obvious history between them.

"Pressley, this is Victoria Lang, an old college friend from my university days."

"We were considerably more than just friends back then," Victoria chuckled with the kind of intimacy that comes from shared memories, then sobered as she surveyed the extensive wreckage around them. "Someone doesn't like you very much. Detective Anderson has already filled us in on the basic details of your investigation, but my partner, Mark Rogers and I would like to hear about everything that's been happening directly from your perspective."

"I'll make some fresh coffee for everyone." Pressley hurried to the break room, partly to be helpful but mostly to give herself a moment to process this unexpected development. Jealousy niggled at her consciousness like an unwelcome visitor. She shouldn't be worried about women from Jackson's past, especially not now when they had much more serious concerns. He was with her now, although they'd never actually put an official label on their relationship. She'd assumed they were romantically involved after their intense experiences during the last case. Had she been mistaken about the nature of their connection?

She filled five ceramic cups with the strong coffee Jackson preferred, arranged packets of sugar and creamer on a serving tray, and carried everything to the small conference room where Jackson had gathered the federal agents and the local detective. The atmosphere felt tense and businesslike. "Where are you in the briefing?"

"I thought it would be appropriate to wait for you before we began." Jackson smiled at her in a way that immediately eased some of her concerns. "Victoria was just telling me that the agency has been conducting their own investigation into The White Veil Society."

"Have you found anything useful?" Pressley took a cup and settled into one of the comfortable chairs around the oval table.

"They're an elusive group, that's certain. One that's been operating successfully for decades without detection." Agent Lang paced the small space with restless energy before sitting directly across from Pressley. "We're working under the assumption that the group consists entirely of women, but we also strongly suspect they may have at least one or two men working as inside informants. Someone with access to local law enforcement or government records."

"Are you suggesting someone in the police department?" Pressley glanced at Detective Anderson, who listened with an increasingly dark expression. "That would certainly explain why no one has been successfully arrested for these murders over all these years. Someone in law enforcement could easily cover up evidence or misdirect investigations."

"You're grasping at straws, Miss Taylor." Mark Rogers, a middle-aged man with graying hair and skeptical eyes, shook his head dismissively. "I don't believe any of the men in this town would be capable of that kind of systematic wrongdoing."

"The murders aren't their only criminal activity," Agent Lang continued, ignoring her partner's objection. "We're uncovering substantial evidence of money laundering operations. A group like this would need significant funding to maintain their activities over such an extended period. Equipment, vehicles, weapons, safe houses—it all costs money."

"Here in Redwood specifically?" Jackson asked, leaning forward with interest.

"Either here or in one of the neighboring communities. Their emotional focus seems to be centered on this town because of that young girl's death back in 1947. They wouldn't want to operate too far from what they consider their spiritual headquarters."

The idea that people could harbor such intense

hatred for so many decades turned Pressley's stomach. A rage so strong and consuming that it would be passed down from generation to generation like some kind of twisted family heirloom.

"The two of you have gotten yourselves involved in something much bigger and more dangerous than a simple murder investigation," Victoria said, her tone carrying both warning and what might have been genuine concern. "This is like poking a spider in the center of its web, and the spider doesn't appreciate being disturbed."

Pressley described in detail the day Mildred had drugged her and locked her in the attic, including her discovery of Lilly's journal and her harrowing escape. "I'm honestly more worried about Jackson's safety than my own. The society has a clear pattern of targeting men."

"You should be worried about yourself as well, Pressley. If you continue to get in their way or pose a significant threat to their operations, you'll be eliminated whether they traditionally kill women or not. Survival will trump ideology every time."

Jackson gripped her hand firmly under the table, his warm touch providing reassurance. "We always look out for each other. Now that federal resources are involved, we can take a step back from the front lines. Let the FBI handle the dangerous aspects of this investigation."

"That assumes you still can step back safely.

Things may have already progressed too far for a simple withdrawal." Victoria steepled her fingers in a gesture that suggested deep thought. "Besides, Jackson, you might be the very key we need to put an end to this organization."

"How exactly do you mean?" Pressley felt a chill of premonition.

"He's a man," the agent said with a slight smile. "If they could be convinced that he's vulnerable and alone, isolated from backup..."

Pressley glared at Jackson with growing understanding and anger. "You told her about your insane idea of being used as bait?"

"Only as a potential last resort if all other avenues fail."

She pushed to her feet abruptly, her chair scraping against the floor. "I'm going to start cleaning up the office. You can finish this discussion without me." She stormed from the room, her footsteps echoing her frustration. He knew exactly how she felt about the dangerous idea of him being used as human bait, and he'd gone behind her back to discuss it with federal agents.

Pressley grabbed an empty storage box from the supply room and began aggressively tossing scattered papers into it, taking some satisfaction in the physical activity. She righted overturned chairs as she moved through the space, replaced displaced drawers with perhaps more force than necessary, and threw anything broken or irreparably damaged into the garbage can.

The furious pace at which she worked helped burn off some of her anger and anxiety. When she'd restored some semblance of order to the main office area, she sat back on her knees, head down, working to steady her breathing and regain her emotional equilibrium.

Hold on. She pulled something small from underneath her desk, a jump drive she didn't recognize. The device was sleek and expensive-looking, not something that belonged to their office. Could one of the people who'd broken in have accidentally dropped it during their destructive rampage?

That seemed too convenient, almost impossibly lucky. Not even the most amateur criminal would be careless enough to leave behind evidence so obviously. She pushed to her feet and headed back to the conference room where the others appeared to be finishing their discussion. "I found this wedged under my desk." She dropped the small device into Agent Lang's outstretched hand, secretly wishing she'd had access to a computer to examine its contents before turning it over to federal custody. "My laptop was stolen, so I wasn't able to analyze what's on it."

"Agent Rogers, would you mind fetching the portable unit from our vehicle?"

"Of course." When he returned moments later, he set a high-end laptop on the conference table and carefully inserted the mysterious jump drive. After a few seconds of loading, he looked up with surprise.

"We have GPS coordinates to what appears to be a warehouse location, detailed information about several offshore banking accounts, and a collection of photographs showing shadowy figures performing some kind of ritual dance in a wooded area."

"Who could have taken these pictures?" Pressley leaned over the agent's shoulder to get a better view of the screen. "Surely The White Veil Society wouldn't document their criminal activities."

"Unless there's a traitor operating within their organization," Agent Lang said thoughtfully as she closed the laptop. "Someone who's finally decided to expose them. We'd like both of you to maintain your planned presence at this weekend's festival because we'll need all available eyes and ears in case these women decide to make an appearance. We'll be in touch with further instructions."

The two federal agents and Detective Anderson gathered their materials and left the office, leaving Pressley and Jackson alone with their thoughts and the lingering tension.

Pressley frowned as she watched their vehicles disappear down the street. "Things certainly got chilly in here after they examined the contents of that jump drive."

Jackson pulled out a small piece of paper and quickly jotted something down. "I memorized the GPS coordinates for that warehouse before they closed the laptop. Want to pay an unofficial visit tonight and see what we can discover on our own?"

"I thought you told the agents we were going to take a step back from active investigation."

"That performance was purely for Victoria's benefit. She tends to want to control every aspect of any operation she's involved in. I only said that to ensure she wouldn't be monitoring our activities too closely."

"Don't you trust her professional judgment?" Pressley studied his face, noting the subtle tension around his eyes.

"Not for a single second." He folded the paper and placed it carefully in his pocket. "This conversation goes no further than this room, Pressley, but Victoria is exactly the type of woman who would either join The White Veil Society or at least sympathize with their cause."

"Why would you think that? She gave me the distinct impression that the two of you were romantically involved during college."

"Not even close to being true. We were assigned to work together on a couple of academic projects, but other than those forced interactions, we barely spoke to each other. She never dated anyone as far as I knew, had no male friends whatsoever. She consistently acted as if men were fundamentally inferior and couldn't be trusted with important decisions." He leaned against the edge of the table. "During our required collaborations on school assignments, she immediately took complete control as if I didn't possess a functioning brain."

Pressley sank into a chair, feeling overwhelmed by these new complications. "If we can't trust the federal agents, who exactly can we rely on? She also seemed to be implying that Anderson might be a corrupt police officer."

"That could be a deliberate misdirection designed to send us on a wild goose chase while we're looking in the wrong direction entirely."

"It's going to be extremely difficult to determine if she's actually a member of the society or simply approves of their methods." The situation had become significantly more complex and dangerous. If Victoria was somehow involved with the killers, she'd be in a perfect position to sabotage their every move. Did she want them at the festival to provide additional surveillance, or to position them where a convenient "accident" could eliminate them? And who had left that jump drive—someone trying to help their investigation or someone trying to lead them into a trap?

Just as Pressley was about to voice these concerns, a tremendous explosion blasted out the front windows of their building and shook the entire structure. The sound was deafening, and the shockwave knocked several items off shelves and sent papers flying.

Jackson dove forward and tackled Pressley to the floor, rolling them both under the solid protection of the conference table. He positioned his body to shield her from any potential debris or secondary explosions. "Are you injured?"

"Other than ringing ears and a sore elbow from when you heroically threw me to the floor, I think I'm fine."

He carefully helped her to her feet and led her to what remained of the front windows. His car was completely engulfed in bright orange flames, with black smoke billowing into the evening sky. The intense heat could be felt even from inside the building. Sirens wailed in the distance, growing steadily louder as emergency responders raced toward their location.

He heaved a resigned sigh as he surveyed the destruction. "I guess we'll be taking your car tonight," he said, unconsciously rubbing his temples where a stress headache was beginning to form.

"You still want to investigate that warehouse after everything that's happened?" Her mouth dropped open in disbelief.

"Absolutely. Now more than ever." He walked over to her car and plucked a sheet of paper from under the windshield wiper. "Another friendly message: 'You won't be warned again.'" He rolled his eyes with dark humor. "They've made that same threat before."

A fire truck pulled into the parking lot with lights flashing and sirens blaring. Firefighters quickly deployed their equipment and aimed powerful streams of water at the blazing vehicle, working to prevent the fire from spreading to the building or other cars.

Pressley turned her attention from the dramatic scene outside to their damaged office. How long would it be before everything they'd worked for went up in flames?

"I'll be right back." Jackson disappeared around the corner of the building, moving with purpose. When he returned a few minutes later, he gestured toward the staircase leading to her upstairs apartment. "You have another laptop up there, correct?"

"Yes, my personal computer."

"The security camera system was damaged in the explosion, but we might be able to recover some footage from the memory card." He took the stairs two at a time, with Pressley following close behind.

She retrieved her personal laptop from the bedroom and set it up on the kitchen table. The familiar domestic setting felt surreal after the violence and chaos of the evening.

Jackson carefully inserted the SIM card he'd recovered from the damaged security camera. "Here we go." After several seconds of digital static and interference, two shadowy figures appeared on the screen. One of them used a tool to pry open the front door while the other kept watch for potential witnesses or interference.

Jackson typed in several commands, and additional footage from inside the office began playing on the screen. The image quality wasn't perfect, but it was clear enough to see the intruders' activities.

"They're both slender in build, definitely consistent with being women," Pressley observed, leaning closer to the screen.

"That matches my assessment exactly."

The two women moved through the office with practiced efficiency, systematically destroying everything in their path. They weren't acting randomly or emotionally. This was a planned operation designed to send a specific message.

One of the intruders suddenly turned directly toward the camera and raised her arm in what might have been a gesture of defiance. As her sleeve fell back, it revealed a distinctive tattoo on her forearm. The same symbolic markings they'd photographed in the ritualistic clearing.

Then, almost deliberately, she appeared to drop something from her pocket and used her foot to kick it under Pressley's desk.

"Look at that. One of them is trying to help us," Pressley said, feeling a surge of hope for the first time in hours. "All we have to do now is figure out who she is and find a way to make contact safely."

Chapter Thirteen

While they drove through the darkening countryside toward the warehouse, Pressley couldn't shake the troubling fact that Jackson didn't trust Agent Lang. The woman had strongly hinted that someone in local law enforcement was on the take, working secretly with the White Veil Society. But if Jackson's suspicions were correct, then who could they possibly trust? The mysterious unknown woman who'd broken into their office and deliberately left behind evidence? The situation felt like trying to navigate through a minefield blindfolded.

Instead of waiting for professional backup, she and Jackson were headed alone to investigate a potentially vacant warehouse listed on a jump drive that may or may not have been intentionally dropped as a means to help them solve the case. Every rational instinct she possessed was screaming that this was a terrible idea. "If Lang does share the ideology of the White Veil

Society, does she know that one of their members might be turning traitor?"

Jackson shrugged, his hands gripping the steering wheel tighter as they turned onto a poorly maintained gravel road. "It's certainly possible. She did demonstrate extensive knowledge about the society before she even arrived in town. Most other law enforcement agencies we've contacted just dismiss the organization as a harmless women's group, since there's never been any concrete evidence linking them directly to the murders."

"Which is exactly the theory someone secretly working with the society would want to promote." Pressley stared out the passenger window at the desolate landscape rolling past them. Abandoned farmhouses and overgrown fields stretched as far as she could see, creating an atmosphere of isolation that made her increasingly uneasy.

"Exactly my thinking." He reached over and gave her hand a quick, reassuring squeeze. "I'm genuinely sorry the FBI involvement didn't provide the solution you'd hoped for."

"I have a really bad feeling about this entire case, Jackson." Her throat felt tight with emotion and growing dread. "I don't want you to become just another statistic, another name added to the list of men who've died because of this vendetta."

He lifted her hand to his lips and pressed a gentle kiss to her knuckles. "I don't plan on being one of their victims, I promise you that."

But those other men hadn't planned on their acts of simple human kindness being the cause of their violent deaths either. Every single one of them had probably believed they were just helping a stranded young woman, never imagining they were walking into a carefully orchestrated trap. "I bet Mildred was the very first girl to play the role of the hitchhiker on prom night."

"You're probably right about that." He returned both hands to the steering wheel as they navigated a particularly rough section of road. "She was certainly attractive enough in her youth, judging from that old photograph on her mantelpiece."

"I had no idea when Nate Duvall first walked into our office that we'd end up trying to solve what amounts to a seventy-year-old urban legend."

Jackson grinned despite the seriousness of their situation. "Makes the whole thing more interesting, doesn't it?"

Interesting? "You're completely crazy."

He laughed, and the sound provided a moment of lightness in the growing darkness. "At least I'm crazy with you."

She wished he would have said crazy about her instead, but this wasn't the time for relationship analysis. "There it is."

The warehouse loomed before them like something out of a massive nightmare, a two-story brick monstrosity that had seen better days. Broken windows stared down at them like dead eyes, the cracked and pothole-filled parking lot was littered with wind-blown garbage, and weeds grew through every crack in the pavement. The entire structure exuded an aura of abandonment and decay.

"This does not look like a suitable meeting place for any kind of organized group." Pressley reluctantly retrieved her weapon from the glove compartment, even though she genuinely disliked carrying a gun. "Are you certain we're at the right coordinates?"

"Positive." He opened his door and slowly slid out of the vehicle, scanning their surroundings for any signs of danger. "I may not be perfect, but I trust my memory completely."

Side by side, they approached the imposing building with careful, measured steps. There wasn't a single other vehicle in sight anywhere around the warehouse, which allowed some of the tension to leave Pressley's shoulders. There couldn't be much immediate danger if they were the only two people here. Still, something about the place made her senses tingle with warning the closer they got to the entrance.

"Stay directly behind me," Jackson instructed as he gripped the handle of the heavy metal door. It opened with a loud, protesting shriek of metal scraping against metal that seemed to echo forever in the stillness.

Pressley glanced nervously over her shoulder at the empty parking lot behind them. Not seeing any movement or signs of life, she stepped carefully into the dark interior of the warehouse and immediately clicked on her heavy-duty flashlight. The beam cut through the darkness, revealing towering stacks of crates and equipment covered in dust and cobwebs. "Should I take the right side of the building while you search the left?"

"That sounds like an efficient plan."

She headed toward a large collection of wooden crates stacked against the far wall. This entire expedition could turn out to be a tremendous waste of time and effort, or they might discover something beneficial to their investigation. She offered a quick, silent prayer for the latter outcome. They needed divine intervention to put an end to the society's decades-long reign of terror in Redwood.

The first crate she examined contained nothing more interesting than reams of standard copy paper, while another held empty manila folders and basic office supplies. It wasn't until she reached a container at the bottom of the stack that things became genuinely intriguing. Inside, she discovered newspapers supposedly dated from the 1940s and 1950s, but the pages were as crisp and fresh as if they'd just rolled off a modern printing press. "Jackson, you need to come see this immediately."

Her continued search also revealed a computer-printed list of what appeared to be names. However, Pressley would have wagered her favorite pair of shoes that every single name on that list was completely fabricated.

Jackson appeared at her shoulder and peered into the crate with growing interest. "What could be the point of creating fake historical newspapers?" He picked up a leather-bound ledger from the bottom of the container. "Everything else in this warehouse shows clear signs of age and neglect, except for the contents of this particular crate."

"Look at this—there's another journal here." Pressley carefully lifted a book that was remarkably similar to the diary they'd discovered in Mildred's attic, and she quickly stuffed it into her bag for later examination.

"Shh." Jackson clicked off his flashlight and motioned for silence.

Pressley did the same, plunging them into near-total darkness. The unmistakable scuff of a shoe sole against concrete echoed from somewhere on the other side of the cavernous room, followed by another careful footstep. Then came the sound of muted whispers—at least two different voices conferring in hushed tones. She instinctively shrank back into the protective shadows between the stacked crates. They had walked straight into a carefully planned trap.

"Follow my lead and stay close," Jackson whispered, taking her hand in his steady grip.

Moving as quietly as possible and keeping behind the cover of crates when they could manage it, they made their way toward what appeared to be an exit door at the far end of the warehouse. Pressley strained her eyes and ears, trying to determine how many people were in the building with them, but the intruders remained frustratingly hidden in the darkness. She carefully pulled her weapon from her bag, her hands trembling slightly with adrenaline.

Jackson tested the door handle only to discover it was securely locked. "Stay close to me," he whispered, then led her toward a flight of metal stairs that presumably led to the second floor.

"We'll be exposed going up those stairs," she hissed. "Sitting ducks."

"Keep your body low, watch where you place your feet, move as quickly as possible, and make no unnecessary noise." He placed his right foot on the first step and gripped the railing with his left hand. After pausing to listen for any sounds from below, he began climbing in a crouch. Pressley stayed as close behind him as she could manage without stepping on his heels.

Halfway up the staircase, the entire metal structure suddenly wobbled and clanged loudly against the wall. Pressley couldn't suppress a small gasp of fear as she clutched desperately at the railing to maintain her balance.

"There they are!" someone shouted from the darkness below, their voice echoing through the warehouse.

"Now we run as fast as we can." Jackson pulled her up the remaining steps.

A gunshot rang out, and a bullet struck the wall directly behind where Pressley had been standing just seconds before. Without stopping to aim carefully, she fired several shots into the darkness at the bottom of the stairs, hoping to discourage their pursuers. On the second floor, multiple rooms branched off from a long, dimly lit hallway. "Which direction should we go?"

"Whichever room offers us a way out—a fire escape, a window without bars, anything."

Another shot rang out from below, and plaster exploded from the wall where the bullet struck, sending sharp fragments flying. Several pieces hit Pressley in the cheek, and she hissed in pain while pressing a hand to her face as she ducked into the nearest available room. Her heart sank when she saw that heavy metal bars covered the single window, completely preventing any possibility of escape.

"Why would they go to all the trouble of luring us here and planting false evidence, only to try to kill us?" She looked up at Jackson with confusion and fear. "We weren't exactly making rapid progress on solving the case. Not fast enough to be a real threat anyway. And those voices I heard downstairs—they belonged to men, not women."

"Professional guns for hire, maybe. People with no personal investment in the society's cause." Jackson peered carefully around the doorframe, checking the hallway. "We can't stay trapped in this room. When I start providing covering fire, I want you to run down that hallway and find us another way out. I'll be right behind you."

"Do you promise me that?"

"I promise. Now go." He stepped boldly into the hallway and began firing systematically at their unseen attackers.

Pressley darted past him, frantically peering into each room she passed while searching for an escape route. *Please, God, show us the way out of this nightmare.*

To her growing despair, all of the rooms she checked had the same heavy bars covering their windows. When she reached the door at the very end of the long hallway, she turned the knob desperately. When it refused to budge, she grabbed the handle with both hands and kicked the door with all her strength. It finally gave way, revealing another set of stairs—these made of concrete rather than metal—that led back down to the first floor. "Jackson!" she called out.

He sprinted toward her, then slammed the door shut behind them and immediately began looking for something to barricade it with. "Do you see anything we can use to block this door?"

"No, there's absolutely nothing up here."

"Then we need to start running again." The sound of pounding feet and angry voices let them know their armed pursuers were getting closer and moving fast.

With Pressley taking the lead this time, they thundered down the concrete stairs as quickly as the dim lighting would allow and burst through another door into what appeared to be a separate section of the warehouse—a back area that had been walled off from the front portion where they'd initially entered.

Jackson quickly grabbed a metal chair from a stack of furniture and jammed it under the door handle at an angle. "This won't hold them for very long, but maybe it'll buy us enough time to find a real way out of here."

Pressley tugged urgently on his sleeve and directed his attention to yet another door across the room. She was beginning to feel like a desperate mouse trapped in an increasingly complex maze with no hope of escape.

The sound of violent banging came from the other side of the barricaded door, and they could see the improvised chair beginning to slide sideways under the pressure.

"We have to find an exit right now." Pressley ducked into what appeared to be a small side room that had probably once served as an employee break area. Unfortunately, there was no way of escape there either.

"Over here!" The sudden sound of glass shattering drew her attention to what looked like a small bathroom.

She stared at the tiny window with dismay. "You'll never fit through that opening."

"But you definitely will." He cupped his hands together to give her a boost.

"I'm not leaving this place without you."

More gunfire suddenly rang out, but this time it

was coming from a completely different direction. Jackson carefully peered around the corner of their hiding place. "The shooting is coming from the other side of the warehouse now."

"Does that mean help has arrived?"

"Let's hope so. Come on." They climbed back up the concrete stairs and carefully made their way down the metal staircase on the other side of the building.

When they finally reached the main floor, they discovered FBI agents Lang and Rogers, along with several local police officers, standing over the motionless bodies of two men wearing black masks.

Agent Lang glanced over at them with what might have been relief. "I'm glad to see you're both still alive."

"How exactly did you know we were here?" Jackson returned his weapon to its holster while Pressley placed hers back in her bag with shaking hands.

"We received an anonymous call to the police station reporting gunshots at this location. I honestly didn't expect to find you here, though. You could easily be lying dead on this floor instead of these two hired gunmen."

"What did you think was happening?" Pressley narrowed her eyes. "Random gang violence? Redwood doesn't have gangs, and from everything I've learned about this town, they rarely experience violence of any kind other than a young man disappearing once a year around prom time. If you didn't think this incident directly involved our investigation, then why didn't you just leave it for the local police to handle?"

Agent Lang focused a hard, calculating gaze on her. "We're here to assist with your case."

"Assistance with the White Veil Society investigation, not random criminal activity."

Lang's smile seemed forced and didn't reach her eyes. "Your partner is quite a wildcat, isn't she, Jackson?"

He immediately put a protective arm around Pressley's waist. "Yes, she is. We were deliberately lured here by false information, Victoria. Over there in that crate, you'll find fabricated newspapers that outline supposed rumors of local police covering up crimes. You'll also discover a list of names that may or may not correspond to real people. Everything in that container is printed on fresh, crisp paper. This entire situation was an elaborate trap designed to eliminate us."

Her smile faded quickly. "Since I took possession of that jump drive, I'd like to know exactly how you obtained the coordinates for this location."

He tapped his temple with evident pride. "Memory, remember? I looked over your shoulder when you were examining the contents and memorized the GPS coordinates."

"You don't trust me?" Her expression of shock and hurt seemed rehearsed and artificial.

"Let's just say I don't know who you are anymore, Agent Lang. Whether I can trust you or not remains to be determined through your actions. Are we free to leave this scene?"

"Not yet. Detective Anderson needs to take your official statements for his report." Her features hardened. "And I don't want you interfering in this federal investigation anymore."

"But you specifically asked us to help provide surveillance at the festival," Pressley interjected.

"We've decided we won't need your assistance after all." She turned her back to them dismissively.

"Why don't you step over there with me?" Detective Anderson motioned with his head toward a more private area. Once they were clearly out of earshot of the federal agents, he said quietly, "We need your help at the festival tomorrow. The more trained eyes we have watching for suspicious activity, the better our chances of preventing violence. But I have to ask—why did you come to this place alone? Agent Lang was right about one thing: you could very easily have been killed here tonight."

"Because I have serious doubts about Agent Lang's honesty and her true motivations regarding this investigation." Jackson glanced meaningfully toward where the FBI agent was conferring with her partner. "I don't trust her to share accurate information with us."

"You don't trust a federal agent?" Anderson's eyes widened with obvious surprise. "But you're the one who contacted the FBI and requested their involvement."

"I called the FBI and asked for assistance. Agent

Lang volunteered to take point on the case."

A range of emotions flickered rapidly across Anderson's weathered face—disbelief, shock, confusion, and finally a growing sense of distrust. "Well, that certainly puts a different perspective on things."

Maybe they could rely on the local detective after all, Pressley thought. At least someone in law enforcement seemed to be genuinely interested in solving these crimes rather than covering them up.

Chapter Fourteen

Later that evening, Pressley climbed the stairs to her apartment above the office, her body aching from the adrenaline crash following their harrowing experience at the warehouse. She changed into comfortable pajamas and made herself a cup of chamomile tea, hoping it would help calm her still-frayed nerves. Finally settling into bed, she scooted her back against the pillows propped against the headboard and carefully opened the mysterious journal they'd discovered.

Pressley hadn't been able to examine the cover clearly in the darkness and chaos of the warehouse, but now, under the warm glow of her bedside lamp, she could see the details clearly. She traced the name "Millie" with her finger, noting how the leather binding was aged but well-preserved, suggesting the journal had been carefully stored for decades.

"How did you end up in that warehouse?" she

wondered aloud, then opened to the first page.

The handwriting was immediately recognizable as Mildred's, though written in a younger, more emotional style than the carefully controlled penmanship she'd seen in recent years.

I killed Tommy, and I don't regret it for a single moment. The agony on Papa's face when he carried Lilly's lifeless body into our living room tore my heart to absolute shreds. Tommy deserved to die for what he did to both of us. Every man except my papa deserves the same fate. - Millie

The entry continued with chilling details of how Mildred had pretended ignorance when her father discovered Lilly's body. She'd forced herself to act shocked and grief-stricken alongside her mother when Papa laid Lilly on the parlor sofa. Mildred described how their father had dropped to his knees beside his youngest daughter and covered his face, his shoulders shaking with silent sobs that seemed to echo through the house.

Their mother had wailed in anguish, covering her head with her kitchen apron in the traditional gesture of mourning. Mildred had forced herself to cry, putting her hand over her mouth and doing her best to appear devastated along with them. But it hadn't been easy to maintain the charade. She'd already done her real crying while dragging Tommy's corpse to Henderson's hog farm in the dark hours before dawn.

Mildred wrote that something fundamental had snapped inside her mind that night. She'd resolved to get revenge on every man in Redwood if necessary, because Lilly had been the absolute joy of the Hensley family. Their parents didn't need to know what their "sweet" daughter had become through her secret affair. In their eyes, she would always remain pure and innocent.

Papa had grabbed the telephone from the kitchen wall and called the sheriff, though Mildred knew it wouldn't accomplish anything useful. The authorities would never discover who had really killed Lilly, because the killer was sitting right there in their living room, playing the role of the grieving sister.

When the sheriff arrived to begin his investigation, Papa had ordered Mildred to go to her room, saying she didn't need to hear the details of what had happened. Instead, she'd slipped out to the burn pile behind their house and tossed in the dress she'd been wearing when Tommy had brutally assaulted her. Her bloodstained nightgown could be secretly washed clean when her parents finally went to bed that night.

Pressley felt sick to her stomach as she read these revelations. She now had all the evidence needed to prove that Mildred had killed Tommy Raney in cold blood. But what other dark secrets would she uncover within the remaining pages of this disturbing journal? She turned to the next entry, which wasn't dated until several months later.

Millie

I haven't been able to hide the pregnancy any longer. Papa finally noticed my growing stomach and took a switch to me for disgracing our family name. I pray every night that I'll die in childbirth or that this unwanted baby inside me will stop growing. If it's born a boy, I swear I'll leave it in the woods for the wild animals.

Pressley's hands trembled as she read about the birth occurring on the anniversary of Lilly's death—the following prom night. Mildred had seen this timing as somehow fitting, since she'd already decided that prom night each year would become a night of reckoning that the people of Redwood would never forget.

The journal described how Mildred had named her daughter Primrose, smoothing the baby's dark hair and whispering promises that no man would ever be allowed to hurt her the way Tommy had hurt both her mother and aunt.

Their mother had entered the birthing room and shooed away the midwife, mentioning that various female cousins had come to see the new baby. Despite the scandal of an unmarried daughter giving birth, the extended family seemed surprisingly supportive. When pressed about the father's identity, Mildred had stated that it didn't matter. She'd fallen in love with her daughter the moment she laid eyes on her, understanding that the innocent child couldn't be held responsible for the circumstances of her conception.

The next entry detailed Mildred's first deliberate murder beyond Tommy's killing. On the following prom night, she'd made sure baby Primrose was sleeping soundly in her crib, then snuck out through the bedroom window she'd once shared with Lilly. Dressed in her white nightgown to evoke the image of her dead sister, she'd run barefoot through the dark trees and onto Highway 365.

A truck horn had blared as the vehicle narrowly missed hitting her. Mildred had stumbled backward, pretending to fall and injure herself, knowing the young man would stop to help her. This would be the beginning of her systematic revenge for what had happened to her family. Any man who drove down Highway 365 on prom night would pay the ultimate price.

She'd moaned and grasped her ankle as if in severe pain. The young man had knelt in the dirt beside her, completely unmindful of his expensive prom suit, asking if he could drive her somewhere safe. With one hand extended as if seeking help to stand, she'd used her other hand to bring a large rock down upon his skull—once, twice, three times until he lay motionless beside her.

Leaving his truck exactly as it was with the engine running and the door hanging open, she'd dragged the young man's body to be buried in a grave she'd already prepared next to Lilly's final resting place.

But then something unexpected had happened. Papa had come outside and discovered her in the act of disposing of the body. His face had darkened with a mixture of horror and understanding as he'd demanded to know what she'd done.

"What needed doing, Papa," she'd replied calmly, leaning on the bloody shovel. She could smell the pungent odor of liquor on his breath. He'd been drinking heavily since Lilly's death.

"You're completely insane." He started to remove his leather belt as if to beat sense into her.

Without hesitation, she'd swung the shovel with all her strength. It had struck his head with a muffled, sickening thud, and Papa had fallen into the fresh grave alongside the young stranger. She'd considered it a fitting place to leave him, then filled the entire grave with dirt.

Horror filled Pressley as she processed these revelations. Mildred was truly evil through and through, her mind completely shattered by Tommy's assault and Lilly's murder. The trauma had left the woman utterly unhinged and homicidal. In the morning, Pressley would turn this journal over to Detective Anderson. He'd finally have everything needed to arrest Mildred and put her away forever.

Several years passed before the next journal entry, which was written in a more mature, calculating style.

Mildred

As I've grown older, it has become increasingly obvious that younger women are needed to successfully lure unsuspecting young men to their deaths. I used Primrose a few times when she reached the appropriate age, but then my foolish daughter fell in love and became pregnant, giving birth to a child she named Amara. By that time, I had convinced several of our female cousins to join me in my righteous quest for revenge, and The White Veil Society was officially born.

Minutes after baby Amara's birth, Primrose hemorrhaged and died, providing me with even more fuel for my burning hatred of the male species. I had long ago abandoned the childish nickname "Millie" and adopted my proper birth name, which is much more suited to a woman of absolute power and influence.

I am indeed powerful. The growing number of bodies buried in our family graveyard serves as testimony to that fact. Dear Mama also rests out there now, having died of what the doctor called a broken heart after Papa seemingly abandoned us and never returned home. Sometimes I suspect Mama might have had some inkling of what I do once each year, but she was wise enough never to say anything directly.

I stared into the sweet, innocent face of my newborn granddaughter after Primrose's death. At first, I wanted nothing to do with the infant who had killed my daughter simply by being born, but then I realized the truth. If some man hadn't planted his seed in Primrose, she wouldn't have died in childbirth. Just as was the case with Primrose's own conception, it was ultimately the man's fault, not the baby's.

I will need someone reliable to carry on my sacred vengeance when I grow too old and frail to continue the work myself. This precious child will learn from her earliest years that men are fundamentally evil creatures who deserve whatever punishment we can deliver. I will watch over her much more carefully than I did with Primrose. No more unwanted pregnancies or romantic entanglements. If our numbers ever start to grow too small, we'll figure out alternative recruitment methods when that time comes.

There were no additional journal entries after that final, chilling passage. It was as if Primrose's death had made further documentation unnecessary, or perhaps Mildred had simply become too busy organizing her growing network of female relatives to continue writing. Pressley closed the book with trembling hands and set it carefully on her nightstand. So much pain and hatred resided within those pages—a glimpse into the twisted mind of a completely insane woman that made her shudder with revulsion.

Pressley rolled onto her side and hugged a pillow tightly to her stomach, trying to process everything she'd learned. Thankfully, she wouldn't have to confront Mildred about these horrific revelations. Detective Anderson could handle that dangerous task. This nightmare was almost over. All those murdered men would finally receive the justice they'd been denied for so many decades, and Jackson would be safe from the society's murderous intentions.

Maybe Redwood wasn't the right place for them to establish their lives and business after all. Could she ever feel secure in a community where such evil had been allowed to flourish for so long?

She woke the next morning to Jackson gently shaking her shoulder. "What time is it?" she asked groggily.

"Nine o'clock." He grinned down at her. "You stayed up late reading, didn't you? I could see the light under your door until almost two in the morning."

"Yes, and it was horrifying." She swung her legs over the side of the bed, still feeling exhausted despite several hours of sleep. "Mildred is a deeply sick woman, Jackson. Everything Detective Anderson needs to arrest her and shut down the entire society is documented within those pages." She nodded toward the journal on her nightstand.

"We'd better get it to him immediately, before it mysteriously disappears. If word gets out that we have something so crucial to the case, there are people who will want it back." He headed toward the kitchen. "I'll make some coffee to go."

After he left her bedroom, Pressley went to shower, her mind still reeling from the journal's revelations and wondering why it had been deliberately placed in that warehouse alongside a collection of obviously fake evidence. Someone had specifically wanted them to find Mildred's confession, someone who knew they couldn't resist investigating those GPS coordinates. But who? Was it Amara, perhaps feeling guilty about her family's crimes? Or someone they had yet to encounter?

She washed her hair, dried off, and got dressed in practical clothes suitable for the festival. Maybe they'd discover more answers during tomorrow's event, when the White Veil Society might finally show themselves.

"What if Agent Lang is with Anderson when we arrive at the station?" she asked as Jackson handed her a travel mug filled with strong coffee.

"We'll simply ask to speak with him privately. Victoria doesn't need to know every detail of our communications with the detective."

"True, but the FBI typically wants to be included in every aspect of a case they're officially working on." She hurried to catch up with him as he strode purposefully toward her car.

"We'll tell her it's a personal matter unrelated to the investigation." He looked at her over the top of the vehicle. "I still don't trust her motives or her agenda. For now, I'm willing to trust Anderson because we have no other choice. Let Victoria develop her information through her own methods."

Pressley nodded in agreement. "It really is almost over, isn't it?"

He grinned with obvious relief. "Yes, it finally is."

Thankfully, Detective Anderson was alone in his office when they arrived at the police station. The building was unusually quiet for a weekday morning, and most of the other officers appeared to be out on patrol or preparing for the festival security details. After they entered Anderson's office, Jackson immediately closed the door behind them.

"What's this about?" The detective frowned and crossed his arms defensively. "I hope you two weren't planning any more unauthorized adventures."

"I found something extremely important at the warehouse yesterday." Pressley placed the leather journal carefully on his desk. "It belonged to Mildred, and it contains detailed confessions about the killings and the formation of The White Veil Society. Everything you need to arrest her and shut down the entire operation."

His frown deepened as he stared at the innocent-looking book. "You should have brought this to me immediately, not taken it home to read like a bedtime story."

"I wasn't entirely sure it was authentic evidence, considering all the other fabricated materials in that crate."

"What makes you certain this one is real?"

"Too many specific details that only the actual killer would know. Too much genuine emotion and psychological insight." Pressley leaned forward earnestly. "I think you should lock this up in your evidence safe immediately, so no one can steal it. This journal represents the only solid evidence we have in this entire case. We need to keep its existence between just the three of us."

Anderson unlocked a desk drawer, carefully placed the journal inside, and relocked it with a decisive click. "I'll read through it thoroughly later today. You did good work, even though you absolutely should not have been at that warehouse in the first place." He looked up at both of them seriously. "I'll see you tomorrow morning at eight o'clock sharp by the gazebo in the town square."

"How are things going with the federal agents?" Jackson asked diplomatically.

Anderson sighed heavily and rubbed his temples. "Agent Lang is like a burr in my sock—constantly irritating and impossible to ignore. She's bossy, condescending, and insists on sticking her nose into every aspect of this investigation."

"Where is she right now?" Pressley glanced nervously toward the door.

"I honestly don't know and don't particularly care at the moment." Anderson's frustration was evident. "You two need to be extremely careful. The one thing I don't want you to do is attempt to confront Mildred Hensley directly."

"We weren't planning on it," Pressley assured him, opening the door to leave.

To her shock, Agent Lang was standing directly outside with her hand raised as if she'd been about to knock. "What's going on in here?" Her eyes narrowed suspiciously. "I'm supposed to be included in every meeting and decision that has anything to do with this case."

"Just a personal consultation," Jackson said smoothly, putting his hand on the small of Pressley's back and guiding her past the federal agent. "We'll see you at the festival tomorrow."

"I specifically told you not to attend that event." Lang's eyes flashed with barely controlled anger.

"And I told them I could use their assistance," Anderson interrupted firmly. His tone left no room for argument.

The office door slammed shut behind them with such force that Pressley jumped. "I definitely wouldn't want to be Detective Anderson right now."

"He's tougher than he looks and can handle himself just fine. I like his suggestion about taking the day off." Jackson's mood seemed to lighten as they walked toward the car. "Let's grab some food from the grocery store and spend the entire day at the lake. We can forget about all this madness for twenty-four hours."

That was honestly the best idea she'd heard in a very long time.

Chapter Fifteen

After a wonderful day spent picnicking by the lake and kayaking on the crystal-clear water with Jackson, Pressley had slept better than she had since Nate Duvall first walked through the door of Hudson and Taylor Investigations. The peaceful interlude had been precisely what they both needed—a chance to reconnect as partners and remind themselves why they worked so well together. Now, in the bright morning sunlight, she squeezed past the temporary barricade that had been erected on Main Street to keep vehicles from driving through the large crowd already gathering for what promised to be Redwood's most controversial festival ever.

The transformation of the normally quiet town square was remarkable. A professional band was tuning their instruments on a makeshift stage positioned just a few yards from the park's historic gazebo, the sound of guitars and drums creating an oddly festive backdrop for what everyone knew was a deeply macabre celebration. Food vendors lined both sides of the street, their colorful awnings and signs advertising everything from funnel cakes to barbecue. Carnival games had been set up between the vendor booths—ring toss, duck pond, and basketball shots—while several bouncy houses provided entertainment for the children whose parents had decided this was appropriate family fun.

Most disturbing of all was a booth that had been set up specifically to sell white veils to tourists, complete with a hand-painted sign that read "Get Your Official Redwood Ghost Veil Here!"

"Considering the tragic circumstances that inspired this festival, that display is tacky," Pressley said, shaking her head in disgust at the woman manning the booth.

The vendor, a heavyset woman in her fifties wearing far too much makeup, glared back defensively. "There's nothing wrong with capitalizing on a local event that brings tourism dollars to our community."

"When real people have died horrible deaths, yes, there's something wrong with it."

Jackson gently took her by the elbow and led her away from the confrontation before it could escalate further. "It's completely pointless to argue with people who refuse to see reason. We're here to keep our eyes open for potential threats, not to convert others to basic human decency."

"You're always the voice of reason in situations

like this."

He laughed, the sound carrying a hint of irony. "Somehow that doesn't sound like much of a compliment."

"It was meant as one." She smiled up at him, then forced herself to focus on the growing crowd around them. Most of the festival attendees were wearing white clothing or accessories, apparently thinking it was part of the theme. "I feel like a blueberry in a bowl of vanilla ice cream wearing this navy-blue suit."

"A very beautiful blueberry," he said warmly, planting a quick kiss on her cheek. "We should look professional and authoritative in case someone needs our help or wants to report something suspicious. Look over there. I can see Victoria and Anderson."

Pressley followed his gaze to where the FBI agent and local detective were standing near the information booth. "They appear to be having a heated discussion. What could have upset them so early in the festival?"

"Whatever it is, it's not our concern. I'd honestly prefer not to deal with that woman at all today if we can avoid it." He steered her toward a vendor selling coffee and breakfast pastries. "Two black coffees, please—one with room for cream and sugar."

"Thanks." Pressley accepted the steaming cup gratefully, then turned her attention back to the job at hand. She needed to stay alert and focused, despite the carnival atmosphere surrounding them.

So far, nothing appeared suspicious or out of the

ordinary. The only veils in sight were being worn by tourists who had visited the tasteless vendor booth, and most of them were middle-aged or elderly visitors rather than the young, dark-haired women they were watching for. It seemed The White Veil Society hadn't yet made their anticipated appearance, though Pressley suspected that could change at any moment.

A sudden scream from somewhere nearby made both investigators tense and reach instinctively for their weapons.

Pressley and Jackson spun toward the sound, adrenaline flooding their systems as they prepared for the worst.

To their relief, they discovered the source was nothing more alarming than a teenage boy who had playfully slipped an ice cube down his girlfriend's shirt. She giggled and slapped him in mock outrage, then ran away from him, clearly inviting him to an innocent game of chase through the crowd. Hopefully, the rest of the day would prove to be equally uneventful, though Pressley's instincts told her that was unlikely.

"Uh-oh." Pressley nudged Jackson's arm to alert him that Agent Lang was approaching their position, notably without her partner Agent Rogers in sight.

"So, you've decided to defy my direct orders," Victoria said, her dark eyes flashing with barely controlled anger.

"We're here specifically because Detective Anderson requested our assistance," Jackson replied calmly, shooting her a quick look before returning his attention to scanning the crowd for potential threats.

"I strongly advise you not to interfere with my federal investigation in any way."

"Our official involvement in this case is finished. We found Ethan Duvall's body, which is what we were originally hired to do. We're only here today to provide additional eyes and ears for crowd surveillance."

Pressley silently applauded Jackson's remarkable composure. Other than a barely noticeable tic in his jaw muscle, an observer would never guess that the federal agent had gotten under his skin. Rather than add fuel to Victoria's obvious irritation, Pressley kept her expression carefully impassive and continued to study the festival crowd.

"Excuse us, Agent Lang." Jackson took Pressley's hand firmly and led her toward the area where the band was now playing some authentic 1940s swing music, the nostalgic melodies drifting over the crowd.

"What did you see that made us need to move?" she asked quietly, glancing around the immediate area.

"Nothing specific. I just needed to get away from her before I said something we'd both regret."

"She bothers you on a personal level, doesn't she? Are you certain there wasn't something romantic between the two of you back in college? I mean, if there was, it's all in the past, but her behavior suggests—"

"There was absolutely nothing between us, romantic or otherwise," Jackson interrupted firmly. "If I spend much more time around her, I might let it slip that I don't trust her motives or her agenda. The woman is clearly on some kind of power trip, and I don't want to add fuel to those flames."

Pressley's attention was suddenly caught by a woman weaving purposefully in and out of the crowd and between the vendor stalls. Something about her movement pattern seemed deliberately evasive. It might be Amara, but from this distance and with the woman's hair partially hidden by a scarf, she couldn't get a clear enough look to be certain. "Let's head over in that direction."

"Did you spot something significant?"

"Maybe." She began moving toward a vendor specializing in handmade soaps, noting that every bar displayed was pure white but featured different fragrances—lavender, rose, vanilla, and others. If she hadn't been working an active investigation, she might have stopped to browse. Artisanal soaps were one of her few indulgences, and she had collected quite a variety in her linen closet over the years.

"You sure you don't want to take a few minutes to shop?" Jackson grinned, clearly aware of her weakness for such products.

"Not right now, but I'm coming back later." She caught another glimpse of the mysterious woman. "That's Amara over there by the fried pickles vendor." Another temptation she might have indulged in under different circumstances. "Wait, I've lost sight of her again."

"I can see her from here. Follow me." Keeping a tight grip on her hand, he began tugging her through the crowd.

Several times during their pursuit, Pressley almost spilled her coffee as they dodged festivalgoers who seemed oblivious to their urgent movement. Children darted between the adults, couples strolled hand-in-hand blocking pathways, and elderly visitors moved at a snail's pace with their walking aids. "Is she heading toward the gazebo?"

"That's what it looks like." Jackson increased their speed, weaving expertly between the obstacles.

Giving up on preserving her coffee, Pressley tossed the cup into a trash can as they hurried past. "Amara!" she called out.

The woman cast a startled glance back over her shoulder, her eyes wide with what looked like fear, and immediately stepped up her pace. This time she veered toward the brick building that housed the park's public restrooms. When she ducked into the women's facility, Pressley pulled her hand free from Jackson's protective grip.

"I'll go after her. There's no other exit from that building, so she's essentially trapped."

"I'll stand guard out here and make sure no one else goes in. Be extremely careful, Pressley."

"I will." She slowly pushed the heavy door open, her senses on high alert. "Amara? You need to come out. We've seen you, and we know you're in here."

"I wanted you to see me." The familiar voice came from one of the stalls, and Amara stepped into view. Her pretty face was creased with worry lines that made her look years older than her actual age. "Did you find my grandmother's journal like I hoped you would?"

"Yes, we found it. You're the one who placed it in that warehouse?"

She nodded gravely. "I had specific orders from the society to plant the fake evidence designed to mislead your investigation, but I decided to leave the journal there as well. I was hoping desperately that you would be curious enough to investigate those coordinates."

"Who exactly gave you those orders about the fake evidence?"

"My grandmother Mildred," she said, hugging her arms protectively around her middle. "But I want out of this nightmare. I've never wanted to be part of this organization, and I've done everything in my power to avoid being used to lure men to their deaths. I haven't always been successful in resisting the pressure, although I can honestly say I've never participated in the actual beatings or killings."

Someone rattled the door handle from outside, testing whether it was locked. Pressley quickly pressed her back against the door to prevent entry. "Just a minute, please," she called out. She turned back to Amara with growing urgency. "Why have you decided to come forward now? What's changed?"

"Things are getting very dangerous within the society. There's a serious power struggle happening, and there are rumors that someone wants to eliminate my grandmother and take her place as the head of the organization. I've been able to persuade Grandmother not to force me to participate in murders, but I don't know if I'll have that same influence with whoever might replace her." She grabbed Pressley's arms desperately. "You have to help me get free from all this. They'll make me pay dearly if they discover I've been secretly helping your investigation."

"We will help you," Pressley promised. "But I need to figure out how to get you to safety without being seen by the wrong people. Stay here and go back into that stall. Lock the door and don't come out until I return."

"About time," complained a middle-aged woman who pushed past Pressley when she exited the restroom.

"Where's Amara?" Jackson glanced at the bathroom door.

Pressley quickly filled him in on everything Amara had revealed. "We need some kind of disguise to get her out of here safely."

"I'll be right back." He sprinted toward the vendor area, returning within minutes with a white veil attached to a baseball cap. "It's the best I could manage on short notice."

"It should work perfectly." She went back inside

and waited until the restroom was empty again except for herself and Amara. "Put this on and tuck all your hair up inside the cap. We'll take you directly to Detective Anderson. He can arrange a safe place for you to stay while this situation gets resolved."

Outside, Jackson and Pressley flanked the frightened young woman as they moved through the crowd. The arrogant, manipulative persona she'd displayed when hiring them to find her nonexistent fiancé had disappeared, replaced by genuine terror.

"There's Anderson over by the gazebo." Jackson pointed toward where a huge crowd had gathered.

As they moved closer, Pressley began catching fragments of whispered conversations about someone being dead. A cold dread began creeping up her spine as the implications sank in.

Detective Anderson spotted them approaching and immediately narrowed his eyes at their disguised companion, though Amara quickly ducked her head to avoid recognition. "You can explain her presence later. Right now, there's something urgent you need to see." He parted the crowd of onlookers and waved them through to the center of the disturbance.

Mildred Hensley lay motionless on the ground in a growing puddle of blood that had flowed from a severe gash on the back of her head. Her eyes stared sightlessly at the sky, and her body was positioned in an unnatural way that suggested violence rather than accident.

"No one claims to have seen or heard anything, of course." Anderson shook his head. "Though with this many people around, that seems highly unlikely."

Amara gasped audibly. "Grandmama," she whispered, the word coming out as a strangled sob.

"Keep quiet." Pressley put a warning hand on her arm. "Don't give yourself away." Whoever had killed Mildred could very well be somewhere in this crowd, watching their reactions. "Is it possible she simply fell and struck her head on something?"

"Highly unlikely," Anderson replied. "The wound is definitely on the back of her skull. She would have had to fall straight backward with considerable force to create that kind of injury. Help me get this crowd to move back so the coroner can get through when he arrives." He gestured toward Amara. "Get her away from here and keep her out of sight."

Maybe their disguise wasn't as effective as they'd hoped. Pressley led Amara to a bench positioned about twenty feet away from the crime scene. "Do not, under any circumstances, leave this bench until I come back for you."

"But I'm completely exposed out here in the open." Amara's voice trembled with fear. "I don't know who killed my grandmother, which means I don't know who I should be afraid of."

"Right now, don't trust anyone except Jackson, Detective Anderson, and me." Pressley hurried back to help push the curious crowd away from the crime scene while also trying to keep a protective eye on Amara.

It didn't take long for FBI Agents Lang and Rogers to arrive and immediately take control of the situation. Anderson diplomatically backed away from the investigation and quietly herded Amara to his squad car. He helped her into the back seat and firmly closed the door, probably the safest location for her at the moment given the circumstances.

After about an hour, most of the crowd had dwindled away to resume enjoying the festival activities, though a core group of people who had been near the gazebo during the critical time period remained. Anderson had ordered them to stay for questioning, and none of them seemed particularly bothered by the fact that Mildred was dead. They appeared more interested in the dramatic circumstances of her death than in mourning her passing. The elderly woman hadn't been well-liked in Redwood, which probably made the investigation more difficult.

Once Mildred's body had been officially photographed, examined, and finally removed by the coroner's team, Pressley and Jackson joined Anderson beside his patrol car. Pressley quickly explained that Amara had been secretly helping their investigation as much as she dared without being discovered by the other society members. "She desperately needs a safe place to stay while this all gets sorted out."

"We'll arrange protective custody with a guard." Anderson motioned to a uniformed police officer and quietly asked him to transport Amara to the station immediately. Once that car had disappeared from view, he marched back toward the group of witnesses he'd detained for questioning. "Let's start interrogating these people systematically. Someone had to have seen something significant, despite their claims to the contrary." Even though the FBI agents were already conducting their interviews, he specifically asked Jackson and Pressley to participate in questioning the remaining witnesses.

Unfortunately, no one seemed to know anything useful. One elderly woman mentioned that she'd noticed Mildred sitting alone in the gazebo earlier, but she hadn't seen her talking to anyone or witnessed anyone approaching her. None of the other witnesses Pressley questioned had anything different to report. Apparently, no one had paid any attention to an old woman sitting by herself.

"This feels like a complete waste of time," Pressley grumbled after her fifth unproductive interview.

"It's standard police procedure," Jackson reminded her. "Sometimes investigators get lucky and someone accidentally reveals something important, or their behavior becomes suspicious under questioning."

A sudden scream tore through the air, much more urgent and terrified than the playful sounds they'd heard earlier. Seconds later, a young woman in her twenties came running frantically in their direction, her face streaked with tears.

"You have to help me," she cried desperately. "Please, someone has to help me find him."

"We'll do everything we can." Jackson shot Pressley a look that clearly said 'help me handle this.'

She stepped forward with her most reassuring smile. "Take a deep breath and tell me exactly what's wrong."

The woman swiped her forearm across her streaming eyes, trying to compose herself enough to speak coherently. "My boyfriend has disappeared. He's been missing for over an hour."

"Where did you last see him?"

"By the public restrooms. He said he'd be right back, but when he didn't come out after twenty minutes, I asked a man to go inside and check on him. The man said there was no one in there at all. I've looked everywhere I can think of."

This was probably just a case of two people getting separated in a large crowd, and her boyfriend was likely searching for her just as frantically. "Let's take you over to the information tent. They might have set up some kind of lost-and-found system for situations like this. He may have already checked in there looking for you."

"But would he have left this behind?" She pulled a cell phone from her jacket pocket with shaking hands. "He never goes anywhere without his phone. It's practically attached to his hand."

"Maybe he accidentally dropped it in the crowd."

"No, that's not what happened. I found it sitting on

a table next to one of the food vendor booths. The woman selling burgers and fries told me she saw him leaving with another woman about an hour ago. She said the woman seemed very distressed or upset about something, and my boyfriend went with her to help. That was over an hour ago, and no one has seen either of them since."

Pressley felt her heart drop into her stomach. Had The White Veil Society decided to abandon their traditional prom night schedule and target a victim during the festival?

Chapter Sixteen

After an unsuccessful and increasingly frustrating search for the missing young man throughout the festival grounds, Jackson drove Pressley to the police station to observe the official interview of Amara. The missing boyfriend case had been turned over to the FBI agents, who had immediately cordoned off the area where he'd last been seen and begun a systematic search. Despite their efforts and those of local law enforcement, no trace of the young man had been found—no witnesses to his departure, no security camera footage, nothing but his abandoned cell phone and the testimony of a single food vendor.

Agent Lang curled her lip in obvious displeasure as they entered the stark interrogation room, but didn't order them to leave. Her tolerance seemed to be wearing thin, but she recognized that their local knowledge and relationship with Amara might be helpful to the federal investigation.

The harsh fluorescent lights flickered intermittently overhead, casting an unflattering pallor over everyone in the windowless room. With Lang and Anderson sitting directly across from a visibly frightened Amara at the metal table, there were no additional chairs available. Jackson and Pressley took up position in the corner, close enough to observe every detail but far enough away to avoid interfering with the official questioning.

"Let's start with basic information. Where are you currently living, Miss Jones?" Lang asked with professional detachment. "If that's even your real name, which I seriously doubt."

"It's not my real name," Amara admitted quietly. "I'm a Hensley by birth. My mother never married before her death, so I carry the family name." She glanced hopefully at Detective Anderson. "Could I possibly have a glass of water, please? My mouth is parched."

Anderson motioned toward the two-way mirror, obviously communicating with whoever was observing from the adjacent room. A couple of minutes later, a uniformed police officer entered, placed a plastic cup of water in front of Amara, and left without speaking.

Lang speared Amara with a hard, calculating gaze. "Anything else you need before we begin this official interview?"

"No, ma'am. Thank you."

"Excellent. I'll ask you again, and this time I want

a complete address." She pressed a button on a small digital recorder positioned in the center of the table. "Where are you currently living?"

Amara rattled off a street address in a voice barely above a whisper, including the apartment number and zip code.

Pressley glanced at Jackson, who nodded almost imperceptibly. She'd learned to rely on his exceptional memory for details, and she knew he'd committed every word to memory for future reference.

"It's been brought to my attention through our investigation that you have been a long-time member of The White Veil Society," Lang continued, her tone becoming more aggressive. "Is this accurate?"

"Since my teens, yes ma'am." Amara's voice was so quiet it was almost inaudible.

"Please speak up clearly, or the recording device will not capture your responses adequately."

Amara cleared her throat nervously and took a sip of water. "Yes, I've been involved since my teens. My grandmother raised me from infancy to be a part of society, the same as my mother before her death, and any female cousins who expressed a desire to join the organization."

"How did your extended family members initially find out about this society? Was there formal recruitment, or was it more informal?"

"Word of mouth at family gatherings mostly. Grandmother would identify young women in the family who she thought had the right temperament and gradually introduce them to our purpose."

"Are there any members who are not biologically related to you or your grandmother?"

Amara shook her head definitively. "A blood connection to the Hensley family line is an absolute requirement for membership. Grandmother was very strict about that policy."

"Yet despite this blood loyalty, you've chosen to betray that sacred connection. Why?" Lang crossed her arms and leaned back in her chair, clearly skeptical of whatever explanation might follow.

"I can't participate in this anymore," Amara said, tears beginning to pour down her cheeks. "I understand why my grandmother killed Tommy Raney after what he did to her and Aunt Lilly. What he did was despicable and unforgivable, but all the others since then—they were completely innocent men who were just trying to help women they believed were in genuine distress. My grandmother's justified hatred for one man somehow poured over and infected all of us. We lost essential parts of ourselves in the process of carrying out her revenge."

"Now that your grandmother is dead, who has assumed leadership of the organization?"

"I honestly don't know if there is a clear leader at this point. With Grandmother gone, I'm hoping and praying that the society will fall apart without her driving force."

Lang folded her hands on the table and stared in tense silence at Amara for several long seconds. "Just like that, you expect decades of carefully cultivated hatred will simply vanish into thin air?"

"I hope so. God in heaven, I really hope so."

Pressley found herself praying silently that it would end just that easily, but was anything involving such deep-rooted violence and trauma ever that simple? Her journalistic instincts told her this was far from over.

Anderson cleared his throat and leaned forward. "Miss Hensley, Amara, if I may call you that. I've had the opportunity to read your grandmother's journal that you helped bring to our attention. Thank you for taking that risk."

Lang sent him a shocked and angry look. "What journal? What are you talking about?"

Deliberately ignoring the federal agent's obvious outrage, Anderson continued. "According to Mildred's own written confession, she killed Tommy Raney by repeatedly beating him over the head with a tree branch. The remains we discovered in the makeshift graveyard outside her house showed that all the male victims died from similar blunt force trauma to the skull. Why was this specific method chosen?"

"I don't know the reasoning behind it. That's how Grandmother wanted it done, and no one questioned her methods."

"I demand to see this journal immediately, Detective," Lang interrupted, high spots of angry color appearing on her pale cheeks. "You had no right to keep such crucial evidence from the FBI agents in charge of this case."

"Feel free to complain to my supervisor," Anderson replied calmly, then flipped through some papers on the table in front of him. "Amara, where does the society typically meet to plan their activities?"

"Usually at my grandmother's house, in the main living room."

"Where do they take the men after they've been lured from the highway?" Lang demanded, her voice growing harsh with impatience. "We don't care about routine social meetings."

Amara visibly jerked at the agent's sharp tone. "Since I refused to participate in the actual luring of victims, I was never told those operational details. Grandmother kept that information restricted to active participants only."

"You expect us to believe that convenient story?"

"It's the absolute truth. I swear it."

"So, you're claiming you've never walked Highway 365 as bait or directly killed a man yourself?"

"No, never." Her tears increased in volume and intensity. "My grandmother might have been disappointed in my refusal, but she ultimately respected my wishes about not participating. None of the society members are ever forced to kill against their conscience."

"Then why did you wait so long to come forward

with information that could have saved lives?" Anderson asked, his voice gentle but persistent.

"I couldn't take the guilt anymore. I knew Ethan Duvall personally—I went to school with his older brother Nate. Ethan was a genuinely nice kid who didn't deserve to die in such a horrible way."

"What specific way are you referring to, Amara?" Anderson tilted his head with interest.

"Beaten to death slowly and methodically."

Lang smiled without any trace of humor. "You claim you don't participate in the murders, yet you seem to know very specific details about how they're carried out, Miss Hensley."

"My grandmother would describe everything to me afterward. She seemed to enjoy reliving the details, and I hated every word of it."

"Why did you hire Hudson and Taylor Investigations under false pretenses?" Anderson asked.

"Grandmother specifically told me to approach them. She wanted to know exactly what they had discovered and how close they were to exposing our organization. When she later sent me and one of the other girls to break into their office and destroy their files, I finally decided it was time to seek help from law enforcement." She hung her head in shame. "I know I should have come forward much sooner, but I was genuinely afraid for my safety. If the society discovers that I've talked to you, they'll lock me up somewhere until they decide what to do with me."

"Lock you up, or kill you?" Lang arched one eyebrow.

"They don't kill women. That's one of their fundamental rules."

Pressley had heard that claim before, but she was beginning to doubt its reliability.

Anderson stood and walked around the table. "We genuinely appreciate you coming forward, Amara, but you are still legally an accessory to multiple murders. The cooperation you've shown us today may influence a judge to give you a lighter sentence, but you will face charges."

"You can't send me to prison." She bolted to her feet in panic. "I'll be killed in there by other inmates."

"I thought you just said the society doesn't kill women," Lang said with a smirk.

"The women in my family love what they do, but the society's protection doesn't extend into the prison system. Family members of the men we've killed might very well be incarcerated there. You have no idea what you're dealing with or how far this network extends."

Anderson took Amara gently by the arm and led her from the room, probably to arrange for her protective custody.

Without sparing even a glance at Pressley and Jackson, Agent Lang followed them out, her jaw set with determination and anger.

"We didn't learn anything significantly new from that interview," Pressley said, exhaling heavily with disappointment. "Except for getting Amara's current address."

"That address might prove more important than you think. But first, we should comb Mildred's house while we have the opportunity. With her dead, we can investigate the property without the risk of being shot at. There has to be some clue as to where the society takes their victims to carry out the actual murders."

"The warehouse we found was too obvious."

"Exactly. They'll have other locations, probably multiple sites to avoid detection."

They were heading toward the exit when Anderson intercepted them in the hallway. "Come into my office for a minute before you leave. Make it quick before Agent Lang decides she needs to monitor our conversation."

They hurried into his cluttered office, and Jackson immediately positioned himself in front of the door. "What's the situation?"

"The town council is planning another absolute fiasco," Anderson said, shaking his head in disgust. "Since the festival drew such large crowds and generated significant revenue, the same group of business owners is now planning something they're calling a summer 'prom' for next month." He made exaggerated finger quotes around the word. "It's the dumbest thing I've ever heard given our current circumstances, but the mayor has already approved it."

Pressley felt her heart sink. "They're going to

create another hunting ground for the society."

"That's exactly my concern. I'm going to have officers patrolling Highway 365 that entire night, and I'd like you to be one of them, Jackson. Your experience and instincts could be invaluable."

Pressley's heart dropped even further. "Absolutely not." She turned to look at Jackson with alarm. "You can't do that. It's far too dangerous."

"The other men who were killed were caught completely unaware," Jackson replied, pulling her close to his side. "I won't be operating under the same disadvantage. Besides, I won't be out there alone, right, Detective?"

"I'll have multiple officers hidden in strategic positions to apprehend any woman in white who approaches the highway. Every man acting as bait will have as much protection as we can possibly provide."

"Then I'll be one of those officers watching the decoys' backs," Pressley declared firmly. She would not be dissuaded from this decision.

"Fine by me. The more experienced people we have involved, the better." Anderson sat back in his chair and studied them. "Are you two planning to search Amara's apartment next?"

"We're going to Mildred's house first," Jackson replied. "With her dead, I'm hoping we can find something that will lead us to the society's actual meeting places and operational headquarters."

"I thought you'd already found that location in the

woods."

"We did, but since we discovered it, they'll have moved to new locations. If we can set up a proper sting operation and arrest the remaining members, there might not be any need to risk lives by patrolling Highway 365 during their summer prom event."

Anderson nodded thoughtfully. "I honestly can't understand how a group of women can stay hidden as effectively as they have for decades. Should I just round up every dark-haired woman under twenty-five in the county? They have to be hiding in plain sight somehow. I'll send a couple of officers over to search Amara's apartment while you're at the Hensley place. Maybe between all of us, we'll find something useful. Good luck."

Jackson held out his hand expectantly for Pressley's car keys as they left the building. "I need to replace my vehicle soon."

"I honestly don't mind us sharing mine." She climbed into the passenger side, noting how the afternoon sun was beginning to cast long shadows across the parking lot. "I really don't like Anderson's idea of using men as human bait. Amara was right about one thing—those women genuinely love what they do, and they've had decades to perfect their methods."

"I'll be fine, Pressley. I promise you that."

She hoped desperately that his confidence was justified.

Mildred had only been dead for one day, but already the house had taken on the unmistakable appearance of vacancy. No lights shone in any of the windows, casting the structure in deep shadows. No elderly woman stood on the porch threatening to shoot them for trespassing. The silence was complete and somehow more ominous than Mildred's hostility had been.

Pressley shuddered as they approached the front door. At least she wouldn't have to worry about being drugged and locked in the attic again. Still, she looked forward to the day when she would never have to see this cursed house again. "I'm not going up into that attic," she stated firmly upon entering the musty interior.

Jackson laughed, the sound echoing strangely in the empty rooms. "I'll handle searching up there and leave the downstairs areas to you."

"You're the best partner a woman could ask for." Pressley headed directly for an antique rolltop desk positioned in the corner of the main living room. After systematically searching through all the drawers, cubbyholes, and hidden compartments, she discovered a small gold key tucked behind a bundle of old letters. "Now what exactly do you unlock?"

The key didn't fit any of the desk drawers she'd already searched. Pressley moved to the larger bedroom, which she assumed had been Mildred's sleeping quarters. The hunting rifle she'd once used to threaten them sat propped menacingly in the corner. An ornate jewelry box sat on the dresser, and a large wooden armoire stood against the far wall, replacing a modern closet, filled with clothes, shoes, and a couple of old-fashioned hats.

Pressley hadn't taken the time during their previous visits to examine the house's furnishings carefully. If she didn't know better, she might have thought she'd stepped back in time to the 1940s when Mildred was a teenager. Everything seemed frozen in that era.

The smaller bedroom contained two twin beds covered with hand-stitched quilts that had faded with age, and another armoire—this one empty of everything except a single white nightgown hanging alone on a wooden hanger. Pressley looked more closely at the dark stains on the back of the garment. Had Lilly been wearing this when she was murdered? What a morbid and disturbing thing to preserve.

"Are you finding anything useful up there?" she called up toward the attic ladder.

"Not yet, but there's decades worth of stuff stored up here. It's going to take time to go through everything systematically. How about you?"

"I found a key, but I'm still trying to figure out what it opens." She returned to Mildred's bedroom and thoroughly searched the armoire, checking every pocket of the dresses hanging there. A small drawer contained undergarments and personal items.

Her attention returned to the jewelry box on the dresser. She slipped the gold key into the keyhole, and it turned smoothly—a perfect fit. Inside, she found only a few pieces of inexpensive costume jewelry. Nothing she would consider valuable enough to require locking up. Pressley huffed in frustration and bit her lip. Maybe the key had initially belonged to something that was lost years ago and had been kept purely as a sentimental memento. But except for preserving her sister's bloodstained nightgown, Mildred hadn't seemed like the type to keep sentimental objects. She'd maintained her home with only the bare necessities for survival.

Plopping onto the edge of the narrow bed, Pressley tried to study the room with fresh eyes. She didn't want to think they'd wasted another entire day searching for clues that didn't exist. They knew who had killed Ethan and why, but now that Mildred was dead, other innocent people would die if they couldn't shut down The White Veil Society completely.

Returning to the rolltop desk, Pressley ran her fingers carefully over and under every shelf and drawer, hoping to discover a secret hiding place or concealed compartment. She'd read enough mystery novels to know that old furniture often contained hidden spaces. Still nothing.

Not really expecting to find anything significant, she methodically checked the bathroom, going so far as to open shampoo bottles and examine the contents of the medicine cabinet. The more she searched without finding anything useful, the more convinced she became that they were wasting precious time.

"I found something interesting," Jackson announced, appearing in the doorway with a thick photo album in his hands. "It's full of photographs of the dead men. Like some kind of sick trophy collection."

"Why would anyone keep something so horrible?" She frowned in disgust. Mildred had been far more disturbed than she'd initially realized. "Is there anything showing the guy who disappeared from the festival?"

"No, but Mildred wouldn't have had time to add his photo. Someone killed her before she could update her collection."

The woman had died in the same brutal manner as her victims—blunt force trauma to the head. But why would someone in her organization turn against her? And who among the society members would have the physical strength and emotional detachment to murder their leader?

"Let me check one last area before we give up. The kitchen might hold something important." Remembering how her mother had once hidden a credit card in the freezer to avoid the temptation of overspending, Pressley opened the freezer compartment of the old refrigerator. She found stacks of frozen venison wrapped in butcher paper and a large container of vanilla ice cream. She doubted anything important would be hidden among the frozen meat.

Jackson set the disturbing photo album on the kitchen table and began systematically opening cabinets and searching through their contents.

Pressley had already examined a ceramic cookie jar and several metal storage canisters when her gaze fell on a grease can sitting near the sink. The old-fashioned type that people used for disposing of cooking fat. She lifted the lid and pulled out a sealed plastic bag that had been carefully rolled to fit inside the narrow container.

"Bingo," she whispered, opening the bag to reveal what appeared to be a property deed. She unfolded the official document and read it carefully. It was the deed to another plot of land owned by the Hensley family, located several miles from the main house.

Anderson would want to see this discovery. They might have finally found the society's true headquarters.

Chapter Seventeen

The summer prom was held in an old, weathered barn that had been transformed for the evening into something almost magical. Fresh straw covered the rough wooden floor, creating a rustic carpet that rustled softly under the dancers' feet. Large hay bales had been strategically positioned around the perimeter to serve as informal seating areas where couples could rest between songs. Hundreds of tiny white lights had been strung across the ancient roof beams, creating a canopy of twinkling stars that cast a warm, romantic glow over the entire space. The barn doors had been thrown wide open to the summer evening, allowing the scent of honeysuckle and fresh-cut grass to mingle with the sounds of laughter and music.

Long tables laden with enough food to feed a small army lined one wall, resembling the elaborate spreads typically found at church socials and community gatherings. Homemade pies, casseroles, fried chicken, and countless other dishes created a buffet that would have made any church congregation proud. The whole scene had a nostalgic, small-town charm that made Pressley wish desperately that she and Jackson were attending under genuinely innocent circumstances rather than as part of an elaborate trap.

"What if no woman in white shows up to flag you down later tonight?" Pressley scanned the crowd of dancers for any signs of suspicious behavior.

"Then we go back to the drawing board and come up with another plan," Jackson replied, his shrewd gaze continuously sweeping the area around them. "But I'd bet money there are one or two society members here right now. They'd want to observe firsthand what kind of law enforcement response their activities have generated."

Pressley followed his gaze to where Agent Lang stood near the refreshment table, her posture rigid with tension. "Lang looks like a coiled snake waiting for the perfect moment to strike. She's been staring at every dark-haired woman under thirty who's walked through those doors tonight."

"Not exactly the epitome of subtlety," Jackson observed dryly.

The evening progressed with agonizing slowness, each song and dance feeling like an elaborate charade. Young couples swayed to romantic ballads while Pressley and Jackson maintained their careful surveillance, hyperaware that danger could materialize at any moment. The irony wasn't lost on either of them that they were surrounded by people celebrating love and community while preparing for what could very well be a deadly confrontation.

Shortly after midnight, when the last song had been played and the final dance completed, the two of them made their way to Pressley's car. The parking area was gradually emptying as couples said their goodbyes and headed home, many of them still laughing and reminiscing about the evening's festivities. Jackson would follow their predetermined plan: drive to her apartment building as if taking her home for the night, then meet her in the back alley where she could secretly climb into the backseat. They might be taking their precautions to an extreme level, but if one of the white-clad women did follow them, she'd assume he was traveling alone and vulnerable.

Jackson pulled up in front of the office building, the streetlamp casting long shadows across the deserted sidewalk. "I'll see you around back in exactly ten minutes."

"I need to change into darker clothes and get my weapon," she said, giving him what she hoped was a reassuring smile despite the fear churning in her stomach. She dashed up the stairs to her apartment, taking them two at a time.

Less than ten minutes later, she crouched near the garbage containers in the narrow alley behind the building, her heart pounding as she waited in the darkness. She breathed a deep sigh of relief when she spotted the familiar headlights of her car approaching.

"Are you ready for this?" Jackson asked, tossing her a dark blanket to hide under.

"Not really, but my desire to put an end to these women's reign of terror outweighs my fear," she replied honestly. She awkwardly folded herself onto the floorboard behind the driver's seat and pulled the blanket over her head, immediately feeling claustrophobic in the confined space. "Make sure to describe everything you see as we drive."

"I promise I will."

"Do you think Lang has any idea what we're planning to do?"

"Only if Anderson told her directly, or if she overheard him discussing it with another officer. I'd like to think he's more careful than that, but you never know."

"Is anyone following us?" She hated being unable to see what was happening around them, feeling completely helpless and dependent on Jackson's observations.

"Not that I can detect. Try to relax as much as possible." He reached over the seat and patted her on the head in a gesture that was meant to be comforting but felt more like he was petting a dog.

She slapped his hand away, unable to suppress a nervous laugh. "I'm not a Golden Retriever."

"Sorry. I'm turning onto Highway 365 now."

Her muscles tensed at the announcement. If a woman in white was indeed walking along this stretch of road, they'd encounter her within the next few miles. Surely the remaining society members realized that law enforcement would set a trap after everything that had happened. Who in their right mind would call a summer dance a "prom" without expecting suspicion? Pressley certainly would have been immediately suspicious of such an obvious setup.

Unless this was a counter-trap, and The White Veil Society wanted them to come to this location. What if they were planning to use her and Jackson to send a brutal message to the entire town? A demonstration that no one could successfully oppose them, not even trained investigators and law enforcement?

"I can practically hear the gears turning in your mind from up here," Jackson said with a hint of amusement in his voice.

"What if the real trap is being set for us rather than the other way around?"

"I've considered that possibility. It's been on my mind all evening."

"So, what should we do if that's the case?"

A sudden crash of thunder drowned out his response, and when the sky quieted again, heavy rain began pelting the car with increasing intensity. "We won't be caught completely unaware like the other victims were," he said once he could be heard again.

"That should give us a significant advantage."

She wished she could share his confidence. "There are some clear plastic ponchos in the glove compartment. They're pretty cheap since I only paid a couple of dollars for them at a camping store, but they might provide some protection if we have to get out of the car in this weather." She'd purchased them years ago during a camping trip with college friends and had simply left them there as emergency supplies.

"You always think ahead about practical details."

"More like once I put something somewhere, it tends to stay there indefinitely."

"We just passed the spot where Ethan supposedly picked up his mysterious passenger. I don't see anything unusual or suspicious."

"Turn around at the next opportunity and make another slow pass."

"If we still don't see anything on the second drive-by, do you want to get out and search the area on foot?"

The prospect terrified her, but she knew it might be necessary. "You expect to find something? We've already searched those woods multiple times and haven't come across any trace of the women."

"No, but we know they operate somewhere in this general area. We just haven't been looking in the right—" He suddenly slowed the vehicle. "I can see something white caught on a tree branch up ahead. I'm going to stop and take a closer look. Stay in the car."

"Absolutely not." She threw off the blanket,

climbed over the seat to retrieve the flimsy ponchos from the glove compartment, then followed him out into the downpour. She was completely soaked by the time she managed to put one of the ponchos on. "Here, take this."

He examined the poncho she wore. "Does that thing provide any protection?"

"Better than nothing."

He swiped water from his hair and pulled the second poncho over his clothes before directing her attention to a piece of white cloth hanging from a low branch. He carefully plucked it free and held it up for her inspection, revealing a dark stain marring the fabric. "This looks like blood to me."

"Do you think a man has already been taken tonight? That fabric looks like it might have come from a dress shirt." The possibility that they were too late to prevent another murder filled her with dread.

"That's a possibility we have to consider." He pocketed the evidence and immediately headed deeper into the dark woods. "Keep your eyes open for tracks, broken branches, anything that might indicate someone passed this way recently."

Any tracks that might have existed would be quickly washed away in the torrential downpour. Pressley wasn't trained in tracking or forensic investigation—she was a journalist who had transitioned into private investigation work. Any signs of passage would have to be extremely obvious for her to notice them.

During their previous expeditions into these woods, they'd caught glimpses of white-clad figures flitting between the trees like ghosts. Tonight, the forest seemed completely deserted. A growing fear filled her that another innocent man had already disappeared despite all their careful planning and preparation.

They trudged through increasingly muddy terrain to reach both of the clearings they'd discovered during their earlier investigations. As they'd suspected, there were no signs that anyone had been in either location recently. The mysterious women had moved their operations elsewhere. The same proved true when they checked the abandoned building they'd found previously.

"Watch where you step," Jackson warned, pointing out a metal contraption partially concealed by fallen leaves on the narrow path.

That was a new addition since their last visit. She immediately stepped back as he used a thick fallen branch to spring what appeared to be some kind of hunting trap.

"I'm starting to get a very uncomfortable feeling that we're being deliberately led somewhere specific," she said, unconsciously moving her hand to rest on the gun in her jacket pocket.

"I'm getting the same feeling." Jackson crouched down to examine something in the churned mud at their feet—a bare footprint small enough to belong to a woman positioned directly next to the clear impression of a man's dress shoe. "Look at this. A man has been taken captive, but he appears to have been walking under his own power at this point rather than being dragged. We have to keep following this trail and see if we can rescue him. We cannot let these women murder another innocent person."

Despite the growing sense of unease that was making her skin crawl, Pressley knew he was right. They couldn't abandon a potential victim if there was even the smallest chance of saving his life. She only wished they could be searching anywhere other than these ominous woods where every instinct screamed that they were walking directly into a carefully prepared trap.

"Here's another torn piece of shirt fabric," Jackson said, picking a small white scrap off a thorny bush. "Whoever they've captured is doing an excellent job of deliberately leaving us a trail to follow."

"Wonderful. Just like Hansel and Gretel leaving breadcrumbs through the forest. Everyone knows how that fairy tale ended."

"Let's pick up our pace as much as the terrain allows. This man doesn't have much time if the society follows their usual pattern." Jackson pushed the hood of his poncho back since the rain had temporarily stopped. "Hopefully, he'll continue leaving clues for us to follow. The heavy rain has washed away any footprints he might have left behind."

"How would this victim know that help was coming? None of the other men received rescue attempts." Pressley also removed her hood and scanned the woods that seemed to be closing in around them with each step. Once again, she couldn't shake the persistent feeling that they were walking straight into a deadly ambush. Still, if someone was genuinely in mortal danger, they couldn't simply turn around and walk away. She sent a silent prayer heavenward for protection—not only for the unknown victim, but also for herself and Jackson. They were dealing with an evil organization that had been perfecting their methods for over sixty years.

Jackson stopped abruptly and knelt to study something on the ground. "This branch on the bush has been broken deliberately, not accidentally."

"How can you possibly tell the difference?" She examined the green twig he was indicating.

"Look how it's been peeled away rather than simply snapped off. See this long, thin strip of outer bark that's been pulled away from the main section? That's a deliberate tracking sign."

She stared at the damaged branch with new understanding. A lengthy piece of the outer bark stretched away from the point where it had been carefully torn. "Where on earth did you learn to read signs like that?"

"My grandfather taught me when I was a kid. He was an avid outdoorsman who believed every man should know how to survive in the wilderness." Jackson straightened and scanned their surroundings with increased vigilance. "Stay as close to me as possible. I have a very bad feeling about what we're walking into."

"Should we consider turning back while we still can?"

He shook his head decisively. "We can't take that chance. There's a life at stake."

"So, we're willing to risk our own lives for someone we don't even know."

He turned to face her directly, his expression serious in the dim light filtering through the trees. "You're right to be concerned. I should take you back to safety, then return alone to continue the search. There's no logical reason for both of us to be in mortal danger."

"No way. I go wherever you go, regardless of the risk involved. We can watch each other's backs and double our chances of survival."

He smiled at her with obvious admiration. "You're a remarkably brave woman, Pressley Taylor."

"Hardly. I'm scared out of my mind."

"And yet you're willing to continue forward because someone might need our help. That's exactly what defines true courage." He gently cupped her cheek before turning to resume following the trail.

They continued trudging through the increasingly treacherous mud until they reached a fork in the narrow path. Two routes stretched ahead of them into the darkness, and choosing incorrectly could mean the difference between life and death for their unknown victim.

"We need to find another clue quickly. If we take the wrong path, whoever we're trying to rescue is a lost cause."

Jackson headed down the left fork while Pressley took the right, both of them scanning carefully for any signs of passage. She examined both sides of her chosen path until she spotted something lying partially buried in a pile of decaying leaves. She bent down and carefully picked up what appeared to be a leather wallet, then opened it with trembling fingers.

Her heart virtually stopped when Detective Anderson's familiar face stared up at her from his official police identification. "Jackson! Get over here right now!"

He rushed to her side, alarm evident in his expression. "How in the world did they manage to capture him?"

The implications were terrifying. If the society could successfully take an experienced police detective, then Jackson was definitely within their reach as well. "This explains why Anderson knew to leave a tracking trail for us. He was aware of our plan to patrol the highway looking for women in white. But if he knew we were coming to this area, why did he allow himself to be captured?"

"Unless he didn't have a choice in the matter. I didn't see any sign of his official vehicle anywhere along the highway."

"Do you think they took him from the summer prom?"

"More likely from his office or home. Somewhere private where they could overpower him without witnesses." Jackson pocketed the wallet grimly. "We're being led into a trap now. Anderson is serving as the bait to draw us deeper into their territory. This group of women wants to eliminate all three of us permanently."

"And we're doing exactly what they want us to do."

"Unfortunately, yes. But the detective is counting on us to attempt a rescue. We'll find a way out of this situation somehow."

"Can you promise me that?" The words sounded strangled, forced from a throat that felt like it was closing with fear. She was asking for a promise he couldn't possibly keep, but his confident response provided some comfort. If anyone could navigate them safely through this nightmare, it would be Jackson.

"I seriously doubt Anderson is in any immediate danger. They'll want to keep him alive until they can deal with all of us at once."

She met his gaze directly. "Then let's call for backup right now." She pulled her cell phone from her jacket pocket, only to discover there was no service signal. How conveniently coincidental. They were entirely on their own.

"Keep checking periodically as we move. We might eventually reach an area with better coverage."

Every few steps, she glanced at her phone screen, hoping desperately for even a single bar of signal strength. She didn't care if someone spotted the glowing screen—The White Veil Society already knew they were coming.

Anderson wouldn't have gone with them willingly under any circumstances. The only way they could have taken him would be at gunpoint or through threats against someone else he cared about. The same psychological pressure was now being applied to Pressley and Jackson. They knew exactly what awaited them deeper in these woods, yet they had no choice but to continue forward. God help them all.

The rain began falling again with renewed intensity. Pressley pulled her hood back into place, though staying dry seemed almost pointless under the circumstances. What did personal comfort matter when they were walking directly into what could only be described as Satan's territory?

Mildred had claimed that the society didn't kill women, but that policy might not extend to female investigators who posed a direct threat to their operations. They would kill Jackson and Anderson without hesitation, then probably lock Pressley away until she either died in captivity or agreed to become one of them. But was joining them even a realistic option? She wasn't related by blood in any way to the Hensley family. So why not kill her along with the men? Why go through the trouble of imprisonment?

Unless they had some other use for her that she couldn't yet imagine.

Her mind continued spinning through increasingly dark possibilities until she thought she might lose her sanity somewhere on this nightmarish trail. She stayed as close to Jackson as physically possible without stepping on his heels or colliding with him, as if proximity alone could somehow keep him safe from harm.

He stopped so suddenly that her face collided with his back. She rubbed her nose and peered around him to see what had caused the abrupt halt.

Agent Victoria Lang stood directly in the middle of the path, a cold smile playing across her lips and a large pistol held steadily in her right hand. "It's about time you arrived, Jackson. I've been waiting here for quite a while, and my patience was beginning to wear thin."

Chapter Eighteen

"Where's Detective Anderson?" Jackson demanded as he stepped protectively in front of Pressley. The gesture seemed to amuse Agent Lang, whose cold smile widened with satisfaction.

"He's waiting for both of you in a safe location, don't worry. Now come along quietly." She motioned with the gun for them to walk ahead of her down the muddy trail. "You're so predictably noble, Jackson. Even back in college, you would always step forward to help someone in trouble, even when it meant putting yourself at serious risk. I knew with absolute certainty that you'd show up here tonight, despite the obvious danger."

"How exactly did you manage to capture Anderson?" Pressley asked, carefully slipping her hand into her jacket pocket to conceal her weapon.

"I need you to hand over that gun right now, Pressley. You too, Jackson. We don't want any unplanned shooting incidents that might complicate things." Once they had reluctantly surrendered their firearms, she continued with obvious satisfaction. "As for Detective Anderson, he was remarkably easy to convince once I applied the right pressure. All I had to do was threaten to start killing innocent people at the summer dance if he didn't cooperate. He's quite the noble public servant. Now start walking."

Pressley frowned as they began moving deeper into the woods. "But why are you involved in this at all? You'rc not related to Mildred or her family."

"Oh, but that's where you're completely wrong," Lang said with evident pride. "It turns out my mother left the fold decades ago, wanting no part of what the organization was doing. The family completely disowned her for her betrayal and never spoke of her again. It's amazing what a person can discover with a simple DNA test and some dedicated genealogical research. Anyway, when I found out I was related to these remarkable women, I knew I wanted to join their cause. Whatever the personal cost might be."

"I should have realized you wouldn't come to a small town like Redwood just to help catch some random killer," Jackson said, his voice tight with anger. "You've always been drawn to bigger, more dramatic situations."

Lang laughed, the sound echoing strangely in the dense forest. "Oh, I think a multigenerational group of serial killer women is quite big enough for anyone to want to tackle, don't you?"

"No offense intended, but you don't physically resemble the other society members we've encountered, and you're far too old to lure young men," Pressley pointed out, shooting a quick glance back over her shoulder.

"You're right about that, but this organization desperately needs strong, competent leadership now that Mildred is permanently out of the picture."

"You killed her?" Pressley's steps faltered as the full implications hit her.

"Of course I did. She was standing directly in my way, and I don't tolerate obstacles to my goals. Pick up the pace, please. I'm getting cold and increasingly wet in this miserable weather."

They trudged through the increasingly rugged terrain for approximately another half hour before finally emerging from the woods onto what appeared to be a seldom-used back road. A dark van waited in the shadows with a woman dressed in white sitting motionless behind the steering wheel, her face barely visible in the dim light.

Lang opened the vehicle's double back doors with practiced efficiency. "Sit down right there on the floor." She pulled several plastic zip ties from her jacket pocket and quickly secured their hands behind their backs with professional skill. "Now scoot all the way inside." Once they had complied, she slammed the doors shut, immediately casting them into complete darkness.

"I don't suppose you happen to be double-jointed?" Jackson asked quietly, his shoulder pressing against Pressley's as the van began moving.

"Unfortunately, no. And I'm not wearing shoes with laces that might be useful. What about you?"

"There's no way I can move my hands from behind my back to the front without breaking something important. Feel around as much as you can for anything we might use to cut through these restraints."

It wasn't an easy task given their limited mobility, but she managed to scoot around the cramped space as much as possible. She fell over several times when the driver took curves too quickly, and her head banged painfully against the metal side of the van during one particularly sharp turn. "Ow! That hurt."

"Are you seriously injured?"

"I think I'm okay." Her searching fingers finally gripped what felt like a nail about three inches long. It wasn't much, but it might serve as a weapon if the opportunity arose. She carefully slipped it into her pocket. "I found a nail. Any luck on your end?"

"There's a screwdriver back here somewhere. Not ideal, but better than nothing."

"I've got the nail secured." Hope that they might escape this nightmare began to fill her chest.

The van gradually slowed and then came to a complete stop, the engine falling silent.

Pressley's heart immediately leaped into her throat as she heard footsteps approaching.

"Don't try anything desperate yet," Jackson whispered urgently. "We've got to focus on trying to save Anderson if he's still alive."

The sobering thought that the detective might already be dead sent chills through her.

The back doors of the van opened with a loud creaking sound. Pressley's eyes slowly adjusted to the night, which seemed blindingly bright compared to the absolute darkness inside the vehicle.

Lang efficiently ushered them out and directed them toward a large, weathered barn that looked like it had seen better decades. A single light glowed through one small, dirty window, suggesting someone was indeed inside.

The interior of the barn was even more ominous than its exterior. Detective Anderson sat tied to a wooden chair in the center of the space, his face so severely beaten that he was barely recognizable as the man they'd worked with just hours earlier. Both of his eyes were swollen nearly shut, his lips were split and bleeding, and his uniform was torn and stained with blood. Despite his terrible condition, he was still conscious and breathing.

He managed to open the one eye that wasn't completely swollen shut and let out what might have been a sigh of relief or resignation. "I tried to leave clear messages for you not to come here," he said with difficulty.

"We didn't get them. No cell service in the woods," Jackson replied grimly as a young woman in white roughly shoved him into another wooden chair and began securing him with thick rope.

"You," the same woman said to Pressley, pointing toward what appeared to be an old horse stall. "Get in there."

"I'd rather stay out here with—"

"Do exactly as she says," Lang interrupted with authority.

Pressley shot her a look that could have melted steel if she'd possessed the power, then reluctantly stepped into the stall. The wooden door immediately closed behind her with a solid thud, and she heard the latch being secured. She turned and found she could barely see over the top of the stall walls.

Lang and the other woman left the barn, turning off the single overhead light and plunging the space into near-total darkness.

Pressley immediately began searching for anything she could use to free herself or help the others. It was going to be up to her to get both men out of this situation before Jackson ended up looking like Anderson, and they were all killed. She'd rather die attempting a rescue than spend the rest of her life imprisoned with a group of insane women trying to brainwash her into their twisted ideology.

She turned and tried to raise her bound hands high

enough to reach the stall latch, but it was positioned too far above her head. Next, she tried repeatedly kicking the door, hoping to break it down through brute force.

"Don't exhaust yourself unnecessarily," Jackson advised from the darkness. "You're the only hope we have of getting out of here alive. Detective, are you seriously injured?"

"Some broken ribs. Missing a couple of teeth." Anderson jerked his head toward a corner of the barn that Pressley couldn't see. "They enjoy using a baseball bat. Tommy Raney was quite the athlete back in his day, and they consider it poetic justice."

"Does anyone from your department know your current location?"

"No one," Anderson replied, clearly exhausted from his ordeal. He allowed his head to hang forward.

"What about Agent Rogers?" Pressley asked while continuing to search for a way to open the stall door.

"Lang told me she sent him on what she called a wild goose chase to another county. According to her, he won't return until sometime tomorrow morning."

Pressley's foot suddenly bumped against something solid buried under the moldy hay that covered the stall floor. She kicked the decaying straw away to reveal a wooden handle that might have belonged to a shovel, pitchfork, or some other farm tool. It could serve as another potential weapon, though it would be tough to wield effectively with her hands bound behind her back.

Where had Lang and her companion gone? Were they deliberately leaving the three prisoners alone as some kind of psychological torture tactic? If so, the strategy was working. Perspiration trickled down Pressley's spine despite the cool temperature, and the humidity from the summer rainstorm left the air feeling thick and oppressive. She sneezed violently as dust from the old hay irritated her sinuses.

A large rat suddenly scurried across the stall wall directly in front of her face. She screamed and jumped backward, her heart hammering.

"Pressley!" Jackson's voice rang out with obvious concern.

"Just a rat," she called back, trying to will her heartbeat to return to something approaching normal. But it immediately sped up again when she heard the barn doors opening with a loud scraping sound. She pressed herself against the stall wall and peered over the top of her wooden prison.

Lang entered the barn flanked by seven women dressed in flowing white gowns, their faces pale and expressionless in the dim light. They formed a perfect semicircle in front of the two bound men like some ritualistic tribunal. The federal agent now held a wooden baseball bat that looked well-used and stained with what might have been blood.

"I have to prove myself worthy before these women will accept me as their legitimate leader," Lang announced with obvious satisfaction. "Nothing personal intended, Jackson." Without warning, she drove the baseball bat directly into his stomach with considerable force.

He grunted in pain and folded forward as much as his restraints would allow. "None taken," he managed to gasp.

Pressley immediately resumed kicking the stall door with renewed desperation. The group of silent women completely ignored her frantic efforts as they watched Lang take her time methodically beating both men. Jackson and Anderson would die if she couldn't find a way to get free. *Please, God, help me save them.*

The old wood finally started to splinter under her repeated assault. Two more powerful kicks and the door hung uselessly from its hinges, the latch destroyed. Now she needed to find a way to free her hands so she could retrieve the wooden handle from the stall floor and use it as a weapon.

She stumbled out of the damaged stall, immediately drawing the attention of several heads that turned to observe her with curious but still impassive expressions. Were they simply interested in seeing what she planned to do? One woman against eight opponents?

An old garden hoe leaned forgotten in one corner of the barn. Pressley dropped to her knees and carefully positioned the tool's sharp metal edge against the plastic zip ties around her wrists, then began sawing back and forth with desperate determination. By the time she'd finally cut through the restraints, her hands were bleeding from multiple cuts caused by the sharp edges, but she was free.

Rather than returning to retrieve the wooden handle from the stall, she grabbed the garden hoe and positioned herself between Lang and the two injured men, ignoring the fresh cut on Jackson's cheek and his rapidly swelling eye.

Lang's lips curled in what might have been amusement. "Such a brave little girl. What exactly do you think you can accomplish against all of us?"

"Let's start with just me and you," Pressley replied, her hands sweating around the wooden handle of her improvised weapon.

"You're no match for a trained FBI agent, Pressley." The woman laughed with genuine humor. "All you're going to do is get yourself seriously injured. Let me finish what I need to do here, then we can all leave this barn and get into some dry clothes."

"I will not stand by and watch you beat these men to death. You're murdering them!" She raised the hoe above her head in a threatening gesture.

"All right then. This should be entertaining." Lang adopted a professional fighting stance that spoke of extensive training.

Pressley managed to block the first swing of the bat and jumped backward, immediately realizing how outmatched she was. What had she been thinking? She had virtually no chance of winning a hand-to-hand combat battle against a trained federal agent with years of tactical experience.

"Watch her eyes, Pressley," Jackson whispered urgently from behind her. "They'll always telegraph the direction she plans to swing next."

She managed to dodge the second attack, focusing intently on Lang's eye movements. The seven silent women in white continued watching like supernatural wraiths, their dark, unblinking gazes beginning to unnerve Pressley almost as much as the physical combat. What would happen if, by some miracle, she won this fight against the woman who wanted to lead them? Would they all converge on her at once? She forced herself to shake away such distracting questions and focus entirely on survival.

The next swing caught her solidly in the shoulder, sending shooting pain through her entire left side. Her left hand went completely numb for several terrifying seconds. Biting back a cry of agony, Pressley leaped forward and swung her weapon with all her remaining strength. The metal edge of the hoe caught Lang in the left thigh, ripping through fabric and skin.

The tension in the barn became almost tangible. The watching women's heads swiveled from Lang to Pressley and back again like spectators at a deadly tennis match, but they remained completely silent.

"First blood to you," Lang said with a grin that held no humor. "I won't be careless enough to let that happen again."

Pressley refused to be drawn into a conversation intended to distract her from the life-or-death struggle. She kept her gaze locked on the federal agent and managed to evade two more vicious strikes before the next one caught her directly behind both knees and sent her crashing to the barn floor.

She rolled desperately out of reach before Lang could deliver a killing blow and struggled back to her feet, fighting against waves of pain. Her left leg threatened to buckle completely under her weight. Fighting against the agony, she shifted as much weight as possible to her right leg. How much longer could she possibly continue this uneven battle?

Another brutal strike to her injured shoulder nearly sent her to the floor again, and black spots danced at the edges of her vision.

"Stay focused, Pressley," Jackson's voice reminded her why she was fighting this seemingly hopeless battle.

Blinking back tears of pain and frustration, she uttered a primal scream of rage and desperation and lunged forward with everything she had left. The garden hoe caught Lang directly in the side with a solid impact.

The federal agent's eyes went wide with shock and pain before she dropped heavily to the barn floor, swinging wildly and ineffectively on her way down.

The seven women in white immediately closed

their circle around Pressley and the fallen agent, stepping over Lang's prone form as if she had suddenly become irrelevant to their purposes. Still maintaining their eerie silence, they kept their dark gazes locked on Pressley with an unsettling intensity.

"You," one of them finally spoke in a voice that seemed to come from another era. "You will be our new leader."

"Not a chance." Pressley leaned on the garden tool while trying to catch her breath. "I'm not a man-hater like you. These two men behind me are genuinely good people who don't deserve the brutal treatment they've received."

The spokesperson tilted her head with an expression that remained completely emotionless. "We did not bring either of these men here tonight. It is not yet time for another ritual sacrifice. She brought them here," the woman said, nodding toward Lang's motionless form, "in a misguided attempt to prove herself worthy of joining us."

"I am one of you!" Lang protested, struggling painfully to get back to her feet. "I'm part of the family bloodline."

The seven women turned as one to face her, their synchronized movement somehow more frightening than anything that had happened so far. "You were not invited to join us," the speaker said with finality. "You killed the one who started our sacred mission. The one who gave us purpose and direction for over seventy years. For that transgression alone, we will never allow you to become one of us."

Lang's mouth dropped open in complete shock. "You're going to let these men walk away alive?"

"Yes." The spokeswoman turned to one of her companions. "Cut their bonds and release them."

"We're going to need transportation back to town," Pressley pointed out. "None of us are in any condition for a several-mile hike through those woods."

"I apologize, but we cannot provide that assistance. We will release you as promised. After that, you are entirely on your own."

Pressley glanced at Jackson and Anderson, both of whom were barely conscious. Neither of them, much less herself, were in any physical condition for such a demanding journey through difficult terrain, especially while dragging Lang along with them. There was no way she would leave the corrupt federal agent behind to escape justice. The woman deserved to spend the rest of her life behind prison bars.

Once his restraints were finally cut, Anderson immediately collapsed to the barn floor, unable to support his weight.

Jackson slumped forward in his chair, his face pale with blood loss and exhaustion.

Pressley dropped to her knees beside Jackson and gently cupped his battered face in her hands. "Are you going to survive this?"

"Yes," he whispered, leaning his bloody forehead

against hers. "Thanks entirely to your courage."

"I couldn't bear the thought of not trying to save you—"

The front and back doors of the barn suddenly burst open, and a team of FBI agents, along with several local police officers, stormed inside with weapons drawn. Agent Rogers marched directly to where Lang lay groaning on the floor. He stood over her with obvious disgust and satisfaction. "I knew you were up to something suspicious. Your story about that emergency in the next county never made sense." He gestured to one of the officers. "Cuff her."

Chapter Nineteen

Adrenaline gone, Pressley sagged the rest of the way, every inch of her body aching. "I'm so not a fighter."

Rogers laughed, admiration shining in his eyes. "Looks to me like you did just fine, Miss Taylor. Once, Agent Lang was one of our best, but you beat her." He sobered and turned to another agent. "Call for an ambulance and round up these women. Their reign of terror is over."

He checked on Anderson. "You still with us, Detective?"

"Hmm."

"Good. Hang in there. Hudson?"

"Okay."

"How did you find us?" Pressley struggled to her feet and sat on a rickety three-legged stool.

"When I couldn't locate Agent Lang—" He shot her a hateful look. "I went to the detective's office and found a lease to a plot of land belonging to the Hensley family. Since I had no record of law enforcement having come out here, I acted on a hunch."

"We're glad you did." Tears welled in her eyes. She didn't have to be strong at that moment. With the threat of death no longer looming over her or Jackson's head, she could let all the emotions she'd struggled to keep at bay come forward.

Sobs racked her body, and she leaned her head on Jackson's knee. "I'm so glad you didn't die."

He chuckled. "Ow. Don't make me laugh, sweetheart, but that makes two of us."

"Did she hurt you bad?"

"I'm hurting—I won't lie, but I'll live. You saved my life." He tilted her face to look up at him. "Thank you."

"I would've died in your place if that's what it took."

"The feeling is mutual." He bent and kissed her while paramedics rushed into the barn and law enforcement took the women in white out.

They loaded Anderson into the ambulance first, then Jackson and Pressley when they refused to ride in the same one as Lang.

Anderson shook his head. "See you at the hospital." He stepped back as the doors were closed.

Pressley kept ahold of Jackson's hand on their way to the hospital. Her gaze fell on Anderson. The man did not look good. Lang had done a lot of damage to the detective. It surprised her that he still breathed. Thank God, he had a chance to live and that Jackson, while hurt, was nowhere near as beaten as Anderson.

She dozed, her head against the wall of the ambulance until they stopped in front of the ER. She remained seated while Anderson, then Jackson were placed on stretchers and wheeled inside. A paramedic helped her down and onto a wheelchair.

"Please put me in the same room as my partner, Jackson Hudson."

"I'll see what I can do, ma'am." The doors whooshed open, and he wheeled her through another set of double doors and up to the nurse's station. "I was told to bring these three straight through, and someone would process them here."

"Yes." The nurse took over pushing Pressley into a room, where thankfully, Jackson lay. She helped Pressley onto a bed. "The doctor will be in as soon as possible. He's more concerned about Detective Anderson at the moment." The nurse opened the door to their room and gasped then leaped back.

Lang, bloody and manic, clutched a pair of surgical scissors in one hand and shoved her way inside. "I will finish what I started."

Jackson rolled off his bed as Pressley did hers. They faced the crazed agent as a united front.

"Get Agent Rogers," Jackson ordered the nurse as he shoved his bed between Lang and the two of them.

She nodded and squeezed out the door, yelling for

help.

Remembering the nail in her pocket, then the screwdriver in Jackson's, she reached for his back pocket and brandished the tool like a knife.

Lang narrowed her eyes. "Seriously? You plan on taking me down with that?"

"It's as good as the scissors in your hand." *Lord, not again.*

The bandage wrapped around her middle showed when Lang approached, and her blouse swung open. "I'm going to prison anyway. I might as well finish you and Anderson off."

"Give it up," Jackson said, leaning heavily on the bed. "The society is finished. It's over."

"It's not over until I say it is."

The door burst open knocking Lang into the bed. Jackson shoved and pinned her against the wall as Rogers, gun in hand, entered the room. "Wrong, Lang," he said. "It's over now."

She screamed and dove over the bed, aiming for his face with the scissors.

He fired.

Eyes wide, she collapsed half on the bed, half off.

"I told you it was over." He motioned to another agent outside the room who entered and rolled the bed away.

"How did she get loose?" Pressley helped Jackson onto her bed.

"She knocked out the nurse who sewed up her

side, grabbed the scissors the nurse used to cut the bandage, and ran in and out of rooms until she found you. Or so a cleaning lady said." He heaved a sigh. "I really wanted her behind bars rather than in a grave, but at least she can't hurt anyone anymore."

"Anderson?" Jackson winced as he settled onto the bed.

"In surgery. Some internal bleeding, a fractured eye socket…Doctor said it's touch and go right now. I'll keep the two of you updated." He left them alone.

"You okay, Pressley?"

"Yes. My knee is bruised, maybe my spine, but I'll survive." She sat in the chair provided for visitors. "I know The Phantom had PTSD, but what caused Agent Lang to snap?" She faced him. "I've never met someone so insane before. How was she in college?"

He shrugged. "Normal, didn't date much, though. Said she wanted to focus on her schooling. I always thought something had happened to her in her past, but I never asked."

"Obviously, insanity runs in the Hensley bloodline." She rubbed her knee. "No sane person enjoys killing." At least it was inconceivable to think so.

A nurse arrived to take Jackson to x-ray, and another to take Pressley. Thankfully, she had nothing broken, just bruises, but was told to take it easy for at least a week.

Back in the room, she dozed until Jackson

returned, a bandage on his cheek, the blood washed away. He told her he had a concussion and five broken ribs. "Better than the alternative," he said.

Agent Rogers joined them. "Mind if I take your statements? Find out everything that happened since you left the prom?"

They filled him in, taking turns with the details. "Any word on Anderson?" Jackson asked.

"He's going to make it, the doctor said. The White Veil Society won't be taking any more lives, thanks to you two. You both would make good agents. Have you ever considered the academy, Jackson, now that you're no longer a police officer?"

He shook his head. "I'm happy where I am." He smiled at Pressley. "There's no better partner than that woman sitting right there."

Pressley's face heated. "No thanks, Agent. I like picking the cases I want to work on."

"Like this one?" He raised his eyebrows.

"This one turned out to be something I never expected."

Rogers stood. "Take care, you two." He shook their hands, then left.

"That's the second cold case we solved." Jackson reached for her hand. "What do you say we focus on those?"

"No more cases from the public?"

"Maybe. Don't you feel great when you solve something no one else could?"

She nodded. "I do. But please, no more murderous cult-type societies."

"I promise." He laughed and pulled her to him. "I think that's a promise I can keep."

"You've kept all your promises so far." She leaned over and kissed him.

Until the next one

First chapter of book one, *Lovers' Lane Murders*

Chapter One

Pressley Taylor pulled the stack of bound papers from her grandmother's trunk. She couldn't believe she'd found the notes about the murders from over seventy years ago. More surprising was the wooden box inside the trunk that held a small pistol. She'd heard stories, knew her grandmother had tried finding out who had killed her friend, but Pressley didn't really think the notes had been kept. It surprised her more to know her sweet grandmother carried a weapon. It always seemed like an urban legend to her. Grandma was incapable of going after a cold-blooded serial killer as a young woman.

Clutching the papers to her chest, she headed down the stairs of the house she'd inherited. At the dining table where she'd shared many holiday meals, she sat down and started reading at the beginning, doing her best to decipher her grandmother's scrawling cursive. She booted up her laptop and started typing the notes for easier reading.

February 22, 1946

"Come on, Jean. We've dated for a while. Stop stringing me along." Danny Harrison put his arm around Jean Daley in hopes of stealing a kiss. "Why do you think I drove all the way out here?"

She placed both hands against his chest and shoved him away. "I'm not that kind of girl." The smile on her face said otherwise.

A twig snapped outside. Her smile faded and her eyes widened. "Did you hear that?"

"Just the sound of my heart beating." He turned her to face him.

"Something's out there," she whispered.

He groaned and pulled away. "You're killing me here." He reached for the key in the ignition. "I might as well take you home if all you're going to do is tease."

The hood of the car slammed up, then down. A large man wearing tan pants, a baggy work shirt, and a pillowcase over his head with holes cut for the eyes, dangled cords in front of the window.

Jean screamed, fumbling for the lock on the door. "Drive, Danny!"

He turned the key over and over to no avail. "Just

give him what he wants." He dug for his wallet, tossed it out the window, then rolled the window up and locked the door.

Jean's screams vibrated in the car. Fear struck her senseless.

The masked man bent and peered through the window, tapping the glass with a thick stick. His eyes glittered in the light of the midnight moon. He raised his arm and slammed the wood hard against the windshield again and again. Jean shrieked with each hit, pressing her back against the seat.

The glass shattered. He reached inside and grabbed Danny by the shirt, pulling him across the jagged shards and across the hood, leaving a trail of blood in his wake. Then he turned toward her and put his finger to his mouth, which only caused Jean to shriek louder. "I don't want to kill you, so do as I say."

He dropped the stick and pulled a gun from his pocket, smashing the weapon multiple times over Danny's head and shoulders until the young man lay limp. Jean fought to open her door. When she succeeded, she fell to the ground, then scrambled for the woods.

A hand gripped her hair and yanked her back, dragging her toward Danny's body. The attacker left her in a limp heap beside her boyfriend.

"Please, don't hurt me." Tears blurred her vision. Her gaze locked on the gun swinging toward her head.

She woke up at some point, her body battered and

bleeding. Gripping the grass around her, she painfully dragged herself away from Danny's body. For some reason she knew her assailant watched from the edge of the trees, telling her to run. Sobbing, she struggled to her feet and staggered away.

A car sat at the end of the road. "Help me." She limped forward and froze as the masked man stepped in front of her.

"Why are you running?"

"You told me to." Her voice shook.

"Liar." He backhanded her, knocking her to the ground.

Darkness overcame her again. When she opened her eyes the second time, the man and the car were gone. Jean hurried down the road.

A farmhouse shone like a mirage in front of her. Sobs choking her, Jean pounded on the door until a man in a bathrobe answered. "Help me." She collapsed at his feet.

Present Day

Pressley didn't think she'd sleep easy that night. She glanced at a yellowed copy of the *Texarkana Gazette* stuck in among her grandmother's notes. **"Sex Maniac Hunted."** She flipped through the pages of notes. Where did it say Jean Daley had been assaulted?

Had the town dealt with not only a serial killer but a rapist? Not finding the answer to her question, she stood and placed her hands on her lower back. She leaned backward, sighing at the loosening pops of her spine.

Organizing these notes would take some time. Pressley couldn't consider heading to Texarkana to investigate until any facts she found were in order. It would be a wild goose chase otherwise, and she'd receive no help from the local police unless she had solid information to give them.

Pressley couldn't take too long, though. Her job had only given her three months to get her grandmother's affairs in order. She planned on allowing herself two weeks to go through the notes and formulate a plan to finish what Grandma had started. Could she do that in such a short time? Why not just quit her job and write that book she'd been thinking about? Grandma had left her a nice inheritance. She could take as long as needed.

She rolled her shoulders and poured herself a glass of wine. Hopefully, it would help clear the vision of the attack by the Phantom, the name given the killer by newspapers.

His first two victims had survived their terrifying ordeal. History informed her those that followed wouldn't be as lucky, one of them being Grandma's friend. Still, Pressley didn't think she would've summoned the bravery needed to discover a killer's identity at the young age of twenty as Grandma had. Yet again, Pressley inherited some of that same backbone, or she wouldn't be digging into the murders at the age of twenty-five.

Having grown up on Grandma's stories from childhood on, Pressley had always wanted to find out what really happened. During the reading of Grandma's will, the lawyer had said that Pressley would find what she needed in an old trunk in the attic, and that Grandma's dying wish was that her granddaughter pick up where she'd left off.

Pressley smiled. She'd found it all right, and it was a doozy. Excitement coursed through her along with the drink. What if she succeeded where local law enforcement and Texas Rangers hadn't? Imagine the book she could write!

Before she could change her mind, she booked a room in a local bed and breakfast in Texarkana. Pressley might as well leave as soon as possible and continue her research where it had all happened. She didn't have much reason to stay in Applewood anyway.

~

The next morning, suitcases, notes, and laptop packed, Pressley made the three-hour drive to where it had all begun. After checking into the B & B, she unpacked and drove to the location of the first attacks just as the sun started to set.

She doubted things looked the same after so long, but she hoped to get a "feel" of the place. Locking the car, she strolled the path described in the newspaper and tried to envision the fear of a sudden attack while parking with one's sweetheart.

Parking. Pressley had stayed so busy with schoolwork in high school that she'd never gone parking. She hadn't dated much in college either. Her grandmother had instilled such fear in her over the events of 1946 that even the thought of being in a car alone with a boy after dark had made her blood run cold. That fear left her missing out on a lot of teenage activities.

Now, she gripped that fear with both hands, fully intending to face and conquer what had imprisoned not only Pressley's grandmother but also Pressley herself.

She ambled past the side of the road, immersing herself in the events of February 22, 1946. Tears blurred her vision as she heard the screams of Danny and Jean.

Headlights illuminated the area before a vehicle pulled behind her car. She shrank back into the shadows, unable to see the driver because of the lights in her eyes.

"Ma'am?" A flashlight replaced the headlights, then clicked off to reveal a police officer. "I received a report of a strange vehicle. May I ask what you're doing out here alone?"

Pressley put a trembling hand to her heart. "Research." She stepped from the shadows and moved closer to her car. "I thought you were… well—"

"The Phantom?" A hint of laughter mingled with his words. "You aren't the first to come looking. This isn't the spot. Follow me." He led her a few yards down the road and off the asphalt. "I've heard it happened here. You do know he's most likely dead by now?" He faced her. "Who are you?"

"Pressley Taylor. My grandmother was friends with one of the victims. She left me copious notes."

He nodded. "I'm Officer Jackson Hudson. I'm familiar with the name from former officers, one of whom was my grandfather. Your grandmother interfered with their investigation a time or two. How's she doing? She'd be what, in her nineties now?"

"Yes, she'd be around the same age as The Phantom if he was still alive."

"Nothing to say he is or isn't." He tilted his head. "Why are you digging this all up again?"

"My grandmother's dying wish was that I find out what happened. I may write a book about it, using her notes. She left enough of an inheritance for me to spend plenty of time searching for the truth." Pressley crossed her arms. "Am I breaking the law by being here?"

"No, just dredging up things best left buried. Go home, Ms. Taylor. Let the dead rest in peace." He turned and marched to his car.

"May I come to the station and ask you questions in the morning?"

"Let it be." He slammed his car door and backed up, turning around in the road before speeding off.

Pressley shrugged. The handsome officer hadn't been pleased at all with her explanation for being in Texarkana. She didn't care. Her goal was to fulfill

Grandma's dying wish with or without the help of local law enforcement.

The question was—why wouldn't the police want to solve the murder, no matter how long ago it happened?

Chapter Two

March 24, 1946

Roger Anderson took Paula Wilson's hand. "You don't have to be home just yet, right?"

"What do you have in mind?" She pressed against his arm.

"A little smooching." He grinned.

"I don't know, Roger. What about the attacks a month ago? That guy's still out there." She shuddered, remembering the newspaper article she'd read. "He's a pervert, too. I read he assaulted that girl."

"We'll stay close to the road. No one would dare bother us when someone could drive by at any time. Besides, I bet he was a vagrant traveling through and is long gone by now."

"Okay," she said reluctantly, glancing around the deserted street. Folks had started staying out later when no murders followed close on the heels of the first one, but there still weren't as many people out as usual. "Just for a little while, though. It's Sunday night, and I have school in the morning."

Roger opened the door for her, then hurried to the driver's side. "I'll make it worth the late hour." He winked and started the car.

True to his word, Roger parked just off the main road, easing some of Paula's worry. She turned sideways in the seat and smiled. "Remember, not too long."

"Just a few kisses." He reached for her, pulling her onto his lap.

They hadn't been kissing long when someone tapped on the window. Paula pulled back and stared into eye holes of a pillowcase. She screamed and launched herself to the passenger side of the seat.

The stranger yanked open Roger's door and dragged him out, forcing Roger to his knees. Paula's fingers slipped off the door handle, tears blurring her vision. She closed her eyes as a shot rang out.

~

Hank Woodrow drove slowly past the parked car, craning to see anyone inside. Not being able to, he stopped and got out of his truck. With a cautious glance around the area, he approached the vehicle. "Hello?" Hank cupped his hands around his eyes and peered through the window. He shrieked and stumbled back.

A young woman lay dead in the front seat, her head

against the far window. A man, wrapped in a blanket, lay dead in the backseat. Seconds later, he jumped in his truck and sped back toward town and the police.

"They're dead." He sagged against the desk of Officer Hudson.

"Slow down. Tell me what you saw." Officer Clyde Hudson grabbed his hat and gun and stepped around the desk.

"Two young people shot dead." Hank gave directions to the scene. "Right there on the side of the road."

"Lead the way, Mr. Woodrow." Clyde dashed for his car and followed the other man to where a dark Plymouth sat. "Stay in your car," he told the other man as he pulled his weapon and approached the parked car.

He didn't need to check for a pulse on either victim. The gunshot in the back of their heads told him they were dead. He stepped back and shined a flashlight around the ground finding the spot where the male had been killed execution-style before being placed in the backseat of the car.

The roar of an engine broke the night's silence. Clyde stepped into the middle of the road in time to see a black Ford speed away. The killer had stayed to watch the aftermath. The officer returned to his car and called the station. "Be on the lookout for a black Ford, make 1941. Time to call in reinforcements. Get the Texas Rangers here. We've got a serial killer on our hands."

"You sure? You don't think it's too soon?" his

captain asked.

"Pretty sure. It's been twenty-one days since the last attack, and this time he killed them. He's escalating." An icy fist gripped Clyde's heart. Would the killer wait another twenty-one days, or would he kill again sooner the next time? This crime was far more violent and daring than the previous one. "The victims are parked on the side of the road, Captain. The killer took a big chance at someone driving by and seeing while he killed them. The male victim isn't a small man. His attacker would have to be on the large side to lift his body into the backseat."

"That narrows it down." The captain's sarcasm dripped across the radio waves.

"It's better than nothing. Over and out." Clyde disconnected and went to secure the crime scene after telling Woodrow to go home and not tell anyone about what he'd seen.

~

Pressley sat at a table in the library and pored over old books that mentioned the murders in 1946. Very little appeared in the newspapers that her grandmother hadn't already written about in her journal. Grandma had been as thorough as possible for a civilian. Very impressive for a young college graduate. She'd given up the search when she married and started having babies, but there were still more unknowns she'd left for Pressley to investigate.

The librarian strolled by, pushing a cartful of books

to be reshelved. "Need any help?"

Pressley rolled her shoulders. "Is there anyone alive that would remember The Phantom murders in 1946?"

"There are a few who come to mind. They all live in the nursing home next to the highway. Mr. Carson, Mr. Marvin, and Mrs. Oglesby, but she has dementia. You'd have to catch her on a good day. Why are you interested in something that happened so long ago?" Her brow furrowed.

"Just a project I'm working on." Pressley smiled. "I'm fascinated with unsolved crimes."

"Do you work in law enforcement?"

"No, I'm a journalist on vacation." She thanked the woman and turned back to the books in front of her. The most popular assumption of the killer's identity was a car thief. That didn't make sense to Pressley, but the murders had stopped upon his arrest. Why go from stealing automobiles to serial killing?

She leaned toward the same conclusion her grandmother had, that the killer was a soldier who'd returned home from the war wounded enough in his head to turn to murder. She straightened in her chair. Maybe he'd suffered a head injury that caused him to turn violent.

Closing the books and leaving them on the table as the librarian had instructed, she grabbed her purse and notes and headed toward the nursing home.

"I'm not sure how much they can tell you," the woman at the front desk of the facility said, "but if they're willing to talk to you, I don't see why you can't ask a few questions. Mrs. Oglesby is having a good day. You might want to start there. But, if they say no, I don't want you pestering them."

"I won't. Thank you." She watched as the woman wrote down the names and room numbers on a sticky note.

"Just follow the signs. We have a fairly simple layout. Lunch will be served soon, and the residents don't like to miss their meals."

Mrs. Oglesby was in the first room. Pressley poked her head in to see a woman in a housedress watching a game show on television. "Ma'am?"

She turned and smiled. "May I help you?"

"My name is Pressley Taylor, and I'm Mary Ann Warren's granddaughter. She married a Mark Clark."

"I knew a Mary Ann Warren once."

Pressley stepped further into the room. "I'm a journalist now. Would you mind if I ask you a few questions?"

"Of course. Sit." She motioned to the one other chair in the room. "It's good to see you, Mary Ann, but you shouldn't be roaming around by yourself. They haven't caught the guy yet, you know."

An interesting turn of affairs. Pressley decided to go along with her. She might recall more if she thought it was still 1946. "I'm being careful." Pressley sat. "Have you heard any new news?"

"Not since he broke into that couple's house." She

leaned close and whispered, "I hear that some of the young men are out looking for the killer themselves. That can't be a good thing."

"I agree. It's too dangerous." She must not have gotten that far in Grandma's notes. "I'd like to find out who killed Sally."

Mrs. Oglesby put a hand over her mouth to stifle a gasp. "Did the fiend get to her too? I think you should let Mr. Hudson handle this, Mary Ann."

"I'm hoping he'll help me." The young Officer Hudson, not the former. "But, the police are tight-lipped on this."

"Of course, they are. The public should stay safely locked out of their way. I daresay it isn't safe for us young people to court anymore. Much better to stay home under the watchful eyes of our parents."

"Who do you think the killer is?"

Her eyes widened. "How would I know? With so many soldiers returning home and businesses up and running again, why it could be anyone passing through."

"But killing every twenty-one days? It has to be a local."

She reached over and patted Pressley's hand. "Find a good boy and settle down. Have babies and leave this to the police."

"Do you think it's a soldier?"

The woman looked shocked. "It couldn't be one of our returning heroes. Where's your head, Mary Ann?"

A bell sounded somewhere in the distance. Mrs. Oglesby grinned. "Time to eat. Will you stay and enjoy a meal with me, Pressley?"

"It would be my pleasure." She waited for the woman to move to a wheelchair, then wheeled her into the hall. "You'll have to show me the way."

"Turn right and follow the hall. Hello, Mr. Carson. This is my friend, Pressley Taylor."

An old man using a walker grinned, a roadmap of wrinkles crossing his face. "You sure are a pretty thing."

"We were just talking about soldiers, weren't we, Mary Ann? Mr. Carson was a soldier, Mr. Marvin, too. Yoo-hoo." She waved at another man who stepped into the hall.

Bowed, he walked without help. He turned, revealing a jagged scar on his left temple. "There's the prettiest girl in the building."

Mrs. Oglesby giggled and patted her hair. "Such flattery. Come and eat with us, you two. Mary Ann is asking questions about the murders."

"Ah." Mr. Marvin nodded. "She's slipped back in time again. She does that a lot."

"I've noticed," Pressley said. "But I would like to ask you all some questions about that time, if you don't mind. I'm a journalist writing a book."

"Best to leave that in the past, Miss." His voice hardened. "That was a terrible time."

"We lost some good friends," Mr. Carson said. "We

don't want to relive it."

"Who do you think killed those people?"

"They caught the guy. It was that thief." He moved away, muttering and shaking his head.

"Now you've gone and upset him." Mr. Miller glared at her. "I don't think I will join you ladies for lunch." He followed his friend.

"I've never known either of them to be rude before," Mrs. Oglesby said. "Perhaps you should leave and come visit another day when they're in a better mood. See if Officer Hudson is coherent enough to talk to you."

Pressley sighed. "You may be right." She continued to the dining room where she left the woman with her friends and returned to the front desk to sign out. Pressley hadn't been aware the former officer resided in the home. If she had, she'd have gone to him first. She shoved open the heavy glass doors to see Officer Hudson approaching. "Hello."

He frowned. "I wasn't aware you knew anyone here."

"Friends of my grandmother's." She grinned. "Did one of the elderly people commit a crime? Is that why you're here?"

"No, I volunteer to serve them the midday meal a few days a week during my lunch hour." He narrowed his eyes. "You wouldn't be asking questions and upsetting them, would you?"

"Guilty as charged. The two gentlemen I spoke with

weren't pleased, and my grandmother's friend asked me to come another time."

"Look, Miss—"

"Call me Pressley."

"Okay. The people who lived through those months in 1946 don't want to be reminded of that horror. Stick to the books for your information."

"A first-hand accounting would be invaluable. I don't think the killer was ever caught, and I want to prove my theory."

"If he wasn't caught, he could still have family living here. Family who wouldn't want it known that their ancestor was a brutal serial killer. That would put you in danger."

www.cynthiahickey.com
Cynthia Hickey is a multi-published and best-selling author of cozy mysteries and romantic suspense/thrillers. She has taught writing at many conferences and small writing retreats. She and her husband run the publishing press, Winged Publications. They live in Arizona and Arkansas, becoming snowbirds with three dogs. They have ten grandchildren who keep them busy and tell everyone they know that "Nana is a writer."

www.ingramcontent.com/pod-product-compliance
Lightning Source LLC
Chambersburg PA
CBHW070438300726
48975CB00007B/1968